The
Roving
Rolls

The Case of the
ROVING
ROLLS

A BRAINS BENTON MYSTERY

by George Wyatt

Based on the characters created by

Charles Spain Verral

Illustrated by AL SCHMIDT

WHITMAN PUBLISHING DIVISION
Western Publishing Company, Inc.
Racine, Wisconsin

Contents

1 Unwashed Alligators

Long time no crime.

That's the way it was in Crestwood. That's the way it had been all summer. That was fine for Crestwood, yes. But it didn't create any stampede for the services of the Benton and Carson International Detective Agency, that's for sure. We'd had about as much business as an iceboat agency on the Amazon.

Me? I'm the Carson in the agency, Jimmy Carson. I didn't mind the shortage of crime so much. I was busy. We'd started football practice and this year it looked like I'd have a good chance of making the Crestwood Junior High team. But my partner—"Brains" Benton—gosh, I thought he'd flip if something big didn't pop. And soon.

Then it did.

You might think that two young boys like Brains and me couldn't do much detecting, but that's where you'd be wrong. You'd know just *how* wrong if you'd been with us on the case that had me hanging by my heels over a cliff and both of us playing hide-and-seek with a man in a fez.

It was Saturday morning, early in September, right after Labor Day, when it all started.

My mother and I had just come back from a conference with Mrs. Willoughby about the Crestwood Garden Club's fall flower show. Now, before you get me wrong, *I* was there because I'm handy with a saw and a piece of wood. The ladies needed some shelves and stuff for the show and Mrs. Willoughby had to tell me exactly what she wanted. What a laugh! I had ended up telling her what she should have. Mrs. W. is okay, but a little on the vague side.

My mother had made me dress in full Sunday uniform for the meeting because Mrs. Willoughby had sent her car and her chauffeur, Frothingham, for us. In spite of his name, Frothingham is a good egg, and I like riding in the "caw," as he calls it. It's a big white Rolls-Royce, gold-trimmed and a zillion years old.

I had hurried upstairs and was about to change my clothes when the phone rang. I had an idea what the call might be and dashed for the stairs. I was about halfway down when my father took the call. Looking over the banister, I could see my father at the phone, his golf bag leaning against his legs.

"Hello. . . . What?" There was a puzzled tone in Dad's voice. "Just a minute . . . say that again!"

He hung up and turned to my mother, standing there, a dish towel in her hands.

"It's that nut-head again. Remember those calls we used to get saying 'The kangaroos have escaped'? Well, what do you think now? *Now* the voice informs me that the alligators need bathing!"

My mother started to laugh.

"I don't think it's funny," Dad said. "I'm going to get to the bottom of these crazy calls. Jimmy! Come down here!"

My heart was in my mouth. That was the secret message. "The alligators need bathing" was X's way of telling me to get over to his house as fast as possible. We'd used "the kangaroos have escaped" in the past for the secret message, but we knew my father was getting suspicious, so Brains was using the new code phrase.

The impatient honking of a car out front saved me. It was Dad's golf partner, and nothing, but nothing, ever held my father up from his appointed rounds of golf. Out he went, banging the door behind him. I breathed a sigh of relief—saved by a golf ball from a serious session of cross-examination.

I broke a couple of records changing out of my good clothes. That message meant something was up.

In the kitchen, I found my mother bustling around as usual.

"Don't you want a snack, Jimmy? We had break-fast awfully early."

There was a glass of milk and a sandwich on the table. I sat down and started galloping through my snack. My mother leaned against the kitchen sink, eye-ing me. She knew something was in the air. But, thank goodness, Mom never did heckle me with a lot of ques-tions like some mothers do. Anyway, she was spooning up her noontime ration of yogurt—her newest diet kick. How anyone could eat that stuff, a sour, gooey, white liquid, was to me a mystery even Benton and Carson could never solve.

"Anything you want me to do, Mom? Before I go out," I asked with my fingers crossed.

"Yes. See if the mail is in the box and bring it to me like a good boy."

I sprinted to the porch and snatched the envelopes from the box. Hastily I shuffled through them. Hey! One for me, from Uncle Ed! I shoved it in my back pocket and raced back to the kitchen. I asked my ques-tion again. "Anything else?" This time I crossed fingers on both hands and then, for extra safety, I crossed my legs, too.

Mom shook her head. "I guess not, Jimmy . . . have a good time." I was at the door when she called, "Use lots of soap." I turned. She had a big smile on her face and a wise twinkle in her eye. Couldn't fool her. She knew that alligator-bathing business was a message for me.

I got away fast, just in case she started asking some embarrassing questions. Fifteen minutes later, I was at Brains' house, four blocks away on Chestnut Drive. I only made one stop.

I took the back way, up the alley, as usual, for secret reasons. That's where the crime laboratory was located. The building had been a coach house back when people still went around in horse-drawn carriages. Now the downstairs was a garage, and the upstairs— well, you should see it someday!

With my bike carefully hidden in the thick bushes which ran around three sides of the building, I looked around, then quickly moved to the north side of the barn. I found the nail, the third one in the fourth board from the bottom. I pressed it.

From a hidden amplifier a mechanically recorded voice said in a whisper, "State your name and business."

"Operative Three," I replied, keeping my voice low. "Official business."

I waited, though I knew what was coming next.

"Give the password."

"The monkeys have no tails in Zamboanga." That was a new password. We changed it every so often, just to be sure no one could get in who was not officially authorized to do so.

With those words, a section of the wall slid silently, magically open, and I shot quickly through the panel. Just as quickly it closed behind me.

It was dark inside, awfully dark, a darkness that seemed to close in on you. And quiet. So quiet my own breathing startled me. Then a bluish light flashed on, casting an eerie illumination through the darkness. The light was attached to the foot of the staircase, but the foot of the staircase was up at the ceiling. Slowly it came down, and I was at the spot where it touched the floor by the time it got there.

I hurried up the stairs just as a panel at the top slid open and the stairs began folding up behind me. Then I was in the room—the crime lab, and as I said, you should see it.

No matter how many times I went into that room, I always got the same scary thrill out of it. It was as clean as a hospital operating room. Along one side, there was a battery of glass-fronted cabinets, and behind the glass were all sorts of needles and graphs and lights. Each cabinet had plenty of dials on it. This was the communications center. Along another wall was a long workbench loaded with all sorts of power tools.

On the third side of the room was the really scientific part of the lab. There were test tubes, bottles containing chemicals and liquids of various colors, and a microscope. Also Brains' latest prize invention. He called it his "Mug-a-Scope," for constructing mug shots of unphotographed criminals.

The Mug-a-Scope was an electric slide viewer. Brains spent all his spare time cutting out black silhouettes of various-shaped ears, noses, head shapes and sizes, small chins, large chins, weak chins and strong chins, thin eyebrows and heavy eyebrows. You'd give him a word description of a suspect, and he'd take his cut-out parts and put together a head in the slide projector. He'd keep changing this nose for that, these ears for those, and so on until he had a face that looked just about like the one you had described to him. It was something, all right.

In one window Brains had built a tiny house, a pigeon cote. It was the latest acquisition in his communications setup—two homing pigeons. I laughed when he got the birds, but he said they might be mighty important if we ever had a total power breakdown in Crestwood, which we had every time there was a bad storm.

The room was empty when I entered it. I kept my eyes on a large mirror on the one side of the room that contained no apparatus. It swung slowly open, and there sat Brains. The mirror was the one-way type. He could look out at you from behind it, but you couldn't see through it.

Brains got up and walked out to his desk. He didn't say anything. He just seated himself, placed his long fingers together, forming a roof peak, and stared at me.

I stared back. He looked funny in his white lab coat with a green fez on his head. The fez looked like an upside-down, oversize ice-cream cone which had been chopped off. It was a present my Uncle Ed had sent Brains.

Uncle Ed got a big boot out of Brains. When he sent him the fez, he wrote, "Sorry, Sherlock. I meant to get you a deerstalker's cap like Holmes always wore, but I haven't been in London lately. Maybe you can use this in one of your disguises."

Brains couldn't have been more pleased, especially since Uncle Ed called him Sherlock.

Uncle Ed had sent all of us presents. I got some foreign coins for my collection, although I liked even better the ten dollars American he slipped in the package, too. My mother, who's his sister, got a gold scimitar-shaped pin. He'd picked it up in a native bazaar in Istanbul. Mom just loves what I call "junk" but what she calls "costume" jewelry.

I could write a book about my Uncle Ed and maybe I will someday. As a flier, he's tops, and he's a darned good uncle, too. He treats you like a grown-up. After he came back from Korea, he lived with us for a while, but he got pretty restless. He became a private pilot, flying other people's personal planes. He kicked around all over the world and ended up—you'd never guess where. In a place called Kassabeba. It's a very small country, but practically saturated in oil. It's ruled by a sort of king, called an "emir." And Uncle Ed was the old Emir's pilot. I say "was" because the old Emir had died not too long ago. My uncle wrote us he was staying on in Kassabeba to fly for the new ruler. We could tell he liked the job, and the country, from the way his letter sounded.

Brains leaned forward, and the red tassel of his fez swung around and fell over his forehead.

"I see that you've just returned from your meeting with our town's esteemed Mrs. Willoughby. But you could have been here ten minutes sooner if you hadn't stopped to practice-kick a football."

"Well," I answered lamely, "there were these kids down at the corner lot . . . I just stopped for a— Hey! How did you know I was at Mrs. W.'s this morning? And while we're at it, how do you know I was kicking a football?"

"Quite elementary, Operative Three. Would you be wearing your good shoes on a Saturday morning unless your mother had forced you into dress clothes? Would she do this except for an occasion requiring that gentlemanly look? You mentioned a job for the Garden Club. The Garden Club means Mrs. Willoughby. Knowing mothers in general and yours in particular, best clothes would be in order when you had to meet a group of women in the town's only mansion."

I looked at my feet. Gee, I'd been in such a hurry when Brains' call came that I'd changed everything but my shoes.

"Now about your having stopped to punt a football. Obviously, to look your best this morning, you polished your shoes before going. But if you will examine the condition of your shoes as of now, you will note that while the left shoe retains its high-polished gleam, the right shoe, on your kicking foot, is dulled, even scratched, from where your toe has propelled the ball into the air."

He had me. He was exactly right. He'd hit the nail right on the head again. Twice. When it came to deduction Brains was a whiz.

But then there wasn't much that Brains wasn't a whiz on. We were the same age and in the same class at school. He was always high on the honor roll, even though he never seemed to study. I scored only so-so in school, making the honor roll once in a while, but I had to plug at it.

Maybe he got his brains from his father, who was a professor at Crestwood College, and his mother, who taught art there. But wherever it came from, he sure had plenty of gray matter in that head of his.

He'd built up the whole crime lab by himself. Of course, it helped that his parents let him do almost anything he wanted to. They gave him the upstairs of the coach house and never entered it once he had taken over.

We'd been partners in this detective-agency business for a couple of years. Brains did most of the thinking. I did most of the doing, the legwork—following suspects, snagging fingerprints, and stuff like that.

I was pretty good at it, too. Maybe that's because I look like most any other kid my age. I was the right height, the right weight, and didn't have any features that made me stand out. My hair's sort of dark brown, my eyes a little darker brown, maybe. There's nothing about my round face that would make anyone stop twice to look at it—a few freckles, that's all.

Not so with Brains, though. He'd never go unnoticed. First off, his hair is the color of a freshly peeled carrot. If it was any brighter red, it would shine in the dark. He has a big nose, thin, but bony. He thinks he looks like Sherlock Holmes, and he does. He has blue eyes, big feet, and is tall and skinny. He seems to flap when he walks.

He's nobody's fool, though. Take football, for example. Brains doesn't play. He's too skinny. But he can dream up the darndest plays. On paper, you wouldn't think they would work. But that's where his practical side comes out. He gives a play to our coach, the coach drills the team in it, and it works every time.

Brains leaned forward, ready to talk, and I shot the question at him, asking him how come the hurry-up alligator message.

"What's up, X? What's the emergency?"

"There is no emergency," he replied calmly. "Only a void, an emptiness."

"What!" I practically howled. "Then why. . . ."

"The time has come for the Benton and Carson International Detective Agency to expand."

"Expand! Why, we haven't done anything in weeks. There hasn't *been* any crime."

"That's just it," Brains went on, his voice still quiet.

"Let me ask you this: What is the *one* word in the title of our detective agency which marks it as unusual?"

I thought about this a minute. "I guess it must be the word 'international.'"

"Exactly. My compliments, Operative Three. You have cut directly to the heart of the matter."

I had?

"Thus far our activities have all been local. It is time we lived up to our agency's name."

"That's all right with me," I said.

"But how?" Brains poked a demanding finger at me. "Just how do we turn up an international mystery in very national Crestwood?"

I pulled up an old chair and flopped in it. Something crinkled and lights flashed in my head.

Maybe I was sitting smack on our first international case!

2 The Letter

Very mysteriously I pulled Uncle Ed's letter out of my hip pocket. Slowly I held it up to the light, then ripped open the end I could see light through, to avoid tearing the letter itself.

"This letter, my good friend X, is from Kassabeba. Just how international can you get?"

"Undoubtedly from your Uncle Ed," Brains commented. What an observation from the great detective! Just how many pen pals did we have in Kassabeba? I made no comment.

I quickly read the first paragraph to myself and my hopes rose. By the time I'd read the second paragraph, I was feeling triumphant.

"Why the smug, cat-who-ate-the-mouse look, Operative Three?" Brains asked.

I couldn't help smiling. I read on for another moment or two, just to increase the mystery and suspense. But then I couldn't hold out any longer.

"Just get a load of this. You want an international case, and I've got it." I held the letter aloft.

"I await your reading of this obviously interesting epistle," Brains said as he leaned back lazily. But I could tell he was plenty excited.

"Okay, then, listen."

Before I started, I cleared my throat, ahemed a couple of times, and settled myself more comfortably in my chair, just to extract the last ounce of enjoyment from keeping Brains waiting. I knew he was edgy to hear what Uncle Ed had written, although you'd never know it from looking at him.

"Dear Jimmy:

"Salaam and greetings from the burning sands of Kassabeba. And believe you me, the heat's on out here. I mean that in more ways than one, as you will see as you read on.

"How's Sherlock Benton these days? I hope the firm of Benton and Carson isn't too busy. I've got a spot of private-eyeing you can do for me."

Brains leaned forward. He was all ears now. This sounded as if we might really have some international sleuthing to do. I went on.

"Something's going on out here. I'm close to it, but can't quite put my finger on it. Anyway, I do know that there's something rotten in Kassabeba."

"A Shakespearean allusion," Brains interrupted. I glared at him and read on.

> "I think part of the answer is either in Crestwood or will be arriving there any day now. I've got to find out what exactly is going on in a hurry. Time's growing short."

Brains unconsciously looked at his watch.

> "Here's the pitch. You know some of the background, but you'd better have a little more fill-in. When the old Emir died (and there's much doubt as to whether his death was natural or unnatural), his half brother Ras-Bey moved in. He took over, using strong-arm methods, and has ruled with an iron hand ever since.
>
> "The rightful heir to this oil-rich country is young Prince Halam, the Emir's only son. However, he was in England, finishing four years at Eton, at the time of his father's mysterious death. Ras-Bey has seen to it that Prince Halam cannot return to Kassabeba and claim the throne. Friends of the old Emir and Halam have tried desperately to get the Prince back here. They have been stopped cold.
>
> "I've stayed on under Ras-Bey primarily so I would be handy to help Prince Halam, one very nice young man. I think Ras-Bey suspects me, but there's not much he can do about it—so far, at least.
>
> "The coronation of the new Emir—a very big deal out here—is coming up soon. Ras-Bey is riding very high, wide, and nasty, and I don't think Prince Halam's got a chance of making the throne. Time's too short."

Brains interrupted. "As I recall," he said, pressing the back of his right hand against his forehead, "the former Emir died sometime early in April. A six-month period must elapse between the death of one Emir and the coronation of his successor—a period of national mourning. Please continue."

Before I did, I did some rapid calculation and figured there wasn't more than three, maybe four weeks, before the coronation was due to take place. Brains, I knew, probably had the time element figured right down to the minute. I continued.

"So, for Halam's safety, and since plans had already been made for him to finish his education in America, it was decided that the Prince would be better off in the U.S. He will continue his studies at Crestwood College and wait for a better time to claim his rightful throne."

Brains' eyebrows shot toward the ceiling at this news. A prince was coming to Crestwood College where Brains' father was a professor!

"According to the last word I had from England, Prince Halam is due to take off for the U.S. and Crestwood about the same day this letter is being mailed to you. But that's not what's troubling me.

"Two characters very close to Ras-Bey have departed this country. From a palace connection of mine, I found out their visas had been stamped for the United States. They may be heading for Crestwood. Just why, I don't know. Ras-Bey wouldn't dare harm the Prince in America, but I know he'll want to keep him away from Kassabeba until after the coronation.

"What I want you sleuths to do is keep those private eyes open for two strangers visiting Crestwood. Find out all you can about them.

"One of these characters is called the Duke—claims to be British. He's tall, lanky, has a long head and a horse face . . ."

"Dolichocephalic," Brains cut in.

"Dolicose-what?" I asked.

"The technical word for a head much longer than it is broad. In other words, 'horse-faced.' "

"That's what Uncle Ed said," I replied. Once in a while I got steamed at Brains when he went too far with his learning.

I glowered, but Brains calmly looked me straight in the eye. He leaned back in his chair and closed his eyes. I read on.

". . . and usually wears black clothes. I don't think you could miss spotting him.

"The other man is a short, round, bouncy guy, looks like a rubber ball with legs. He's called Jujab. His face is moon-shaped."

"Brachycephalic," Brains cut in again.

This time I didn't dignify his interruption with a question. If that other word meant horse-faced, this word must mean moon-faced. Then I figured that naturally, with the Mug-a-Scope invention, Brains must have studied up on technical names for faces and heads and things.

> "You won't have any trouble spotting him, either. He wears a long, waxed, handlebar moustache. He's very proud of it.
>
> "Anyway, keep your eyes and ears wide open. Report to me anything you can dig up on these guys if they show in Crestwood. Don't try to tangle with them. Just get the facts.
>
> "Best of luck."

The letter was signed "Uncle Ed" in big, sprawling letters.

I sat back, waiting for Brains' comment. I felt like crowing. Little old James Carson had come up with a genuine international mystery. I expected Brains to jump up and shake my hand or slap me on the back or *something*.

Instead, he arose, took off his lab coat and fez, and walked over to a window. He stood there staring out, and I knew his mind was racing. Finally he turned.

"Operative Three, if those two men—the Duke and Jujab—are already in Crestwood, would it not be highly likely that they would seek out a compatriot, a fellow citizen of Kassabeba?"

"Gee, I suppose so. But there aren't any more Kassabebans in Crestwood than a hen has teeth."

"Ah, you forget," Brains said, a wise smile on his V-shaped face. "Who rules the kitchen at the Willoughby mansion?"

The gears in my mind meshed. "You mean that wild man, that . . . that temperamental Turk?"

"Not a Turk, Operative Three. The cook is a Kassabeban, brought by Mrs. Willoughby to Crestwood because of her love for the succulent dishes of the Near East."

Creeps! I'd had a brush with that crazy cook once, and I'll never forget it. I'd made myself a promise to starve to death before I'd ever enter the Willoughby kitchen again.

Then I heard Brains saying, "Come, Operative Three. We wend our way to Mrs. Willoughby's to improve our foreign relations with Kassabeba."

3 The Roving Rolls

It was just after twelve o'clock noon when we slipped out of the crime lab. My brain churned, trying to come up with some excuse to get out of visiting Mrs. Willoughby's cook. Brains, with that keen perception of his, sensed I was holding back.

"Do I detect some hesitancy on the part of my partner?" he asked. "Is such a *simple* thing as a visit to a cook causing you alarm? A detective must take chances, Operative Three. Fear has no place in an investigator's makeup."

"Is that so?" I said to myself, remembering plenty of times on other cases when Brains had been scared and had lit out on his frightened legs as fast as he could. I've got to admit, though, that I was always right with him—most often in front of him.

When he called visiting that Kassabeban cook a simple thing, my thoughts flashed back to a year ago. *Simple!* Ha! Had Brains ever been chased around a hot stove by a furious madman with a meat cleaver in his hand?

That's what happened to me the first and, I hoped, the last time I was in that kitchen. I was innocent, too. My mother's a great one, you know, for this garden club activity. So, this one afternoon a year ago, she had me bike out to Mrs. Willoughby's with some huckleberry leaves to go along with some fancy flower arrangement Mrs. W. was dreaming up. "Dream," did I say? It turned out to be a nightmare for me.

I walked into the kitchen—some kitchen. It was all shiny, with glistening pots and pans hanging from the walls. Herbs were strung all over the place. It smelled like a spice factory. In the center of this big kitchen was a long, heavy table. The top of it was as thick as a butcher's chopping block. In the middle of the table were some more leaves.

The cook was standing over a hot stove and hardly gave me a glance when I came in. He was wearing one of those tall chef's hats and a long white apron. He bulged from the middle and bristled from the face. He had long mustachios that drooped down on either side of his chin like an upside-down U. I wondered how he kept them out of the soup.

Anyway, I walked over to the table and plopped my leaves down on top of the other ones.

That started it. You'd have thought I'd tossed a stick of dynamite into a pan of hash the way things started flying around that kitchen.

This chef let out a high, piercing howl, followed by a string of words that were just gibberish to me. He jumped up and down. Then he grabbed a pan. The pan came hurtling through the air, end over end, right at my head. I ducked. When I looked up, here came this crazy cook, meat cleaver in hand, and I knew it was *my* neck, not a chicken's, he was after.

I made for the door in an Olympic record broad jump. I just made it. I could still hear that cook's angry shouts halfway down the driveway as I pedaled for dear life, and I do mean "dear life," since I'm pretty fond of my personal breathing.

I learned later what my crime had been. Those other leaves that I had put the huckleberry leaves on top of were vine leaves—grape vine leaves. It seems that vine leaves are as precious as ten-dollar bills to a Kassabeban. They pickle them somehow, then, when they're soggy as wet rags, they roll them around rice and meat and stuff. I say "ick," but they like 'em.

Mrs. W. even gave some to my mother once. I tasted just one. The Kassabebans can have them. Give me a roast-beef sandwich and a dill pickle any time.

Now you see why I don't consider a visit to Mrs. W.'s kitchen very *simple*.

Brains was crossing the backyard between the crime lab and his house to get his bike. Mine was hidden in the hedge. So, what could I do but head for it? Where X goes, Operative Three is bound to follow.

Then I got a reprieve. Mrs. Ray, the Bentons' housekeeper, showed up at the back door.

"Barclay Benton," she said, in her usual tone of annoyance when she spoke to Brains. "Now, just where do you think you're going? Don't you ever think about eating? You waste all morning in that foolish laboratory of yours, then when it comes time to eat, off you go. Well, let me tell you, Master Barclay—you're not stepping one foot out of this yard until you've had your lunch."

Oh, boy! You can see Mrs. Ray doesn't approve of Brains' detective activities or hardly anything he does. But when she calls him *Master* Barclay, she's really got the steam up. She knows how he hates to be called *Master*.

"Why, Mrs. Ray," Brains called back, smooth as ice cream, "how could you ever imagine that I would forgo the opportunity to partake of any of the tempting concoctions you skillfully prepare? I was just—"

Mrs. Ray cut Brains off. She was one of the few people who could.

"Now, don't you be giving me any of that soft-soap talk with those fancy words of yours."

Brains hadn't fooled her completely, but I could tell from her tone of voice that he had partly soothed her.

"Your lunch will be ready in five minutes," she said and went back into the kitchen.

I was relieved. But Brains wasn't to be put off.

"Operative Three," he said, walking over to meet me. "Once I've had my snack in our kitchen, we head for the Willoughby kitchen."

"Now, wait a minute, X," I cut in. I had just remembered another way out. I have a paper route for the *Crestwood Daily Ledger*. On Saturdays it comes out early, around one o'clock. That's so it can print football and baseball lineups before game time when the local teams play.

"I've got my paper route to do."

Brains frowned and looked at his watch. "Takes you about two hours, doesn't it? All right, then, I'll meet you at Mrs. Willoughby's at three o'clock." With that, he turned and walked toward his house.

He didn't even give me a chance to answer. Not that it would have done me much good. Brains was stubborn when he had an idea in mind. I knew where I was going to be at three o'clock, whether I liked it or not.

So, two-thirty found me biking north on Washington Avenue, heading for the Willoughby mansion. Washington Avenue runs out of Crestwood and becomes the highway to Middlebury. Toll House Road runs off the highway to the east. It's a little-used road these days. Before the highway was built, though, it skirted the eastern edge of Lake Carmine and was the main road to Middlebury. The highway goes around the western end of Carmine and is a shorter, faster route.

The Willoughby mansion is off Toll House Road, in the foothills of the Little Elk Mountains. It's some place, too. There's about a mile of winding driveway from Toll House Road up to the pillared front and portico entrance of the Willoughby house. Those pillars are really something. There are six of them, white and tapered to the top, where they support an overhanging roof. Mrs. Willoughby had originally come from the South, and when the house was built, she had it made like her old southern plantation home.

The Willoughby estate is about four miles from Crestwood. It has gardens with birdbaths stuck all over the place and a fish pond with a statue of a big fish spilling water out of its mouth. There are stables in the rear of the house, but Mrs. Willoughby doesn't keep horses anymore. To the right of the house there's a four-car garage with a two-room apartment over it for the chauffeur.

I turned off Toll House Road into the driveway which winds up to the mansion. And when I say "wind," I mean it really winds. The guy who laid it out must have liked snakes.

Just as I was rounding the first of these S curves, I saw Mrs. Willoughby's Rolls-Royce coming toward me, rounding the curve just ahead. I hopped off my bike and walked it over to the side of the driveway. There was plenty of room; the driveway's plenty wide. Usually, when Frothingham—he's Mrs. W.'s chauffeur, you know—and I bumped into each other, he'd stop for what he called a "bit of chitchat."

I liked talking to Froth. He wasn't a bit stuck-up, even if he did sound that way. The way he spoke English sure wasn't the way I spoke it. Maybe he'd learn if he stayed in this country long enough.

When the Rolls was about twenty-five feet away, I raised my hand to wave.

Creeps! There wasn't anybody to wave to! There wasn't anyone at the wheel. The Rolls was running away. No driver!

I stood there, my mouth hanging down to my chest. Suddenly the Rolls swerved toward me. It didn't slow up. It was aimed right at me!

Boy, did I ever jump back fast!

The Rolls flashed by me, swinging back into the center of the driveway, and headed for Toll House Road. I dropped my bike and took off after it, shouting, running as fast as I could. I just knew the Rolls was going to shoot across Toll House and crash into the ditch on the other side.

Then, when it reached Toll House, it slowed and made a perfect left turn!

Now, the Rolls is a great car, but it isn't human. *Creeps!* It must be haunted!

4 Chrysanthemums and Sour Cream

You could have knocked me over with a soda straw!

I tore down to Toll House Road just in time to see that white Rolls disappearing round a bend, heading toward Lake Carmine.

Brains and I have been up against lots of puzzling and mysterious problems, but this one took all the marbles. How could a driverless car keep from careening off the road? Remote-controlled? I didn't think so.

I sure wished right then that Brains was with me. He'd have some answer. But he wasn't with me, although I expected him anytime. "Besides," I couldn't help muttering to myself, "*this* time I'll have him stumped."

As I was standing there, wondering if I was out of my mind and seeing things, I heard a noise from behind

me. I jumped around like a frightened cat. I guess I was a little spooked.

Looking up the Willoughby driveway, I saw Frothingham coming toward me at jet speed. Only he wasn't in a plane. He was riding Mrs. W.'s English bike. I'd have laughed if I wasn't already so mixed up by what was going on. Here came Frothingham, his knees pumping up and down like pistons. He was in his butler's uniform—he buttled as well as chauffeured for Mrs. Willoughby—and what a sight! He was wearing those morning trousers, I think they're called—gray with a thin black stripe—a white shirt with a high stiff collar, and a cutaway coat—black, and what he calls a bowler hat—I call it a derby.

Frothingham hit Toll House Road at full speed. He tried to turn, but he was going too fast. The bike skittered out from underneath him, and Froth did a swan dive toward the ditch. He landed head and bowler hanging over the edge, his highly polished black shoes and long legs sticking out in the tall grass between the road and the ditch.

"Froth! Froth!" I yelled. "You all right?" I ran over to the ditch. Froth didn't move. I dropped to my knees and grabbed his shoulders. I thought he might have broken his neck.

He groaned. I sighed with relief. He'd just had the wind knocked out of him.

In a minute, Froth, with me tugging at his shoulders, backed his body out of the ditch. He groaned a couple of times more, then stood up. First thing he did was brush off his clothes. Then he looked at me through dazed eyes.

"In which direction did Madame's car go?" Those were his first words.

Gosh! He thought more about that car than he did about himself.

"You all right, Froth?" I asked.

"The car, m'boy, the car? Must overtake it, at once!"

"On a *bike*?" I asked back.

"There's no time. Must pursue it."

"It went that way," I replied, pointing up the road.

Frothingham trotted over to Mrs. W.'s bike. It hadn't been damaged. He was picking it up, ready to set out after the Rolls.

"Look, Froth"—I put a hand on his arm—"it can't get far. There wasn't anyone driving it."

Froth looked at me as if my belfry was filled with bats.

"That, m'boy, is impossible. It was parked in the driveway with the hand brake set."

"Maybe the brake was defective or something. Maybe it just didn't hold, and the Rolls just started rolling away."

When I said that, Froth reacted as if someone had slapped him in the face with a glove, like a challenge to a duel.

He drew himself up, shoulders erect, his long legs straddling the bike seat.

"My dear boy, there has never been such a thing as a defective Rolls-Royce. Not even the most minute part has ever failed to function properly."

"Not in any of them?" This was too much. "You know, every once in a while a car slips off the assembly line with something wrong with it."

Froth was really indignant now.

"Assembly line! Never! The Rolls is made with the loving care of skilled hands. Never has an other than perfect car left the factory."

I guess I must have looked a little skeptical because Froth continued.

"I repeat to you the famous remark made by one of the founders of the company, Sir Henry Royce. He said many years ago, and I quote him word for word: 'It is impossible for us to make a bad car. The doorman wouldn't let it go out!' "

"Okay. Okay, Froth," I sputtered. "I apologize, I apologize. No pistols at dawn."

"But enough of this dillying and dallying," Froth said. "I must recover Madame's car." He started pedaling down the road.

"Wait, Froth. I'll go with you."

Froth kept right on pedaling. I ran back up the driveway, got my bike, and set off after him.

I hadn't gone very far when I heard a shout behind me. *Now what,* I thought. I turned, still picking up speed to overtake Froth. Here came Brains. I signaled him to follow.

As I gained on Froth, Brains inched up on me. After about a mile, the three of us were neck and neck. After another mile, we leaned to the left as we rounded another curve and braked fast.

There was the Rolls, parked by the side of the road. We all hopped off our bikes and ran over to it. I don't know what Brains and Froth expected to see, but a real live ghost inside wouldn't have surprised me any.

The Rolls was empty, undamaged, unattended, and unexplained.

Froth, his face set in a deep, worried frown, started going over that car as carefully as my sister Ann reads a letter from her boyfriend. I felt Brains tugging at my arm. He pulled me aside.

"You seem to have had quite a time for yourself, Operative Three. I think you had better bring me up to date."

I did. I babbled out the whole crazy story in a hushed voice.

"No driver, you say?"

"That's right, Operative X, no driver."

"But that's impossible. Instead of 'seeing things,' you were *not* seeing things." Brains was twisting old sayings—and me—again.

"Well," I said, "put some of that famous brainpower of yours to work on the mystery. I'd like to see what you can come up with."

Brains gave me a look that I guess was supposed to make me feel like I'd gone off my rocker a little.

"I'll give you the conclusion I have reached, but later. Now, let us join Frothingham in his inspection of the car."

Can you tie that? Here Brains had already figured out how a driverless car could make a sharp turn, follow a winding road, and end up safely parked. But does he tell me? No. It's times like this when I can get real burned up at my partner.

We joined Frothingham.

"There seems to be little or no damage," Frothingham said. "But I can't fathom how it got here or who was driving it."

Brains shot a look at me, and for a moment I thought he was going to go on about how I didn't think there was a driver. I felt easier when he didn't.

"Frothingham," Brains said, "the mystery of how the car got here and who was driving it is unimportant as of now. What is important, I firmly believe, is that the theft of the Rolls is the beginning of a serious chain reaction that can have far-reaching, even international consequences."

What a speech!

Frothingham's eyebrows lifted slightly. "International consequences?"

"Yes. Tell me, have you seen any suspicious characters lurking around Mrs. Willoughby's estate? Particularly within the past day or two?"

"Can't say that I have, m'boy." He pronounced the first word "cawnt."

"No, I don't suppose you would. They would be certain to remain out of your sight."

Brains' next question didn't seem to make any sense at all.

"You do all the marketing for the household, do you not?"

Now, what kind of a question was that? Even Froth seemed to think Brains was going a bit off the trolley. I should have known he was leading up to something important.

"Well, yes, m'boy. 'S'matter of fact, I do."

"Then tell me this: Has your cook asked for any additional groceries or unusual types of food lately?"

"Khouri?"

That was the cook's name.

"Well, now, let me ponder the question." Frothingham pondered. "I say there, perhaps you *have* stroked the nail right on the button."

Brains craned his head forward. He was all ears.

"Just yesterday and again today, Khouri had me fetch a quart—a full quart, mind you—of sour cream."

"Two quarts of sour cream in two days," Brain said. "That's a lot of sour cream."

"Too blooming much, if you ask me," Froth replied. His upper lip curled in distaste.

Brains turned to me.

"We must continue our original mission."

Now, just what did two quarts of sour cream have to do with our paying a visit to Khouri? I didn't get it.

"I will elucidate later, Operative Three," Brains said to me in a whisper. We never called ourselves by our code names in front of people, when they could hear us.

Brains was sure building up this mystery, and I didn't even know what the mystery was yet.

"I wonder if you boys would be good enough to help me put Madame's cycle in the boot?" Froth asked.

In the boot? Stuff a bicycle in a boot? Who was wearing boots, anyhow?

"Why, gladly, Froth," Brains said. "I'll get the bike. You open it up."

This I wanted to see. Brains must have figured Froth's fall had knocked him a little silly. "Humoring him, I'll bet," I said to myself. I followed Froth as he moved to the rear of the Rolls. He took out a key and unlocked the trunk compartment. Brains pushed the bike over, and they lifted it in.

Brains smiled at the question marks on my face. "What we call the trunk in a car, the English call a 'boot.' " I shook my head.

As I was walking over to my bike, just to the left of the left front fender—I wonder what they call a fender —I saw some fresh-cut flowers by the side of the Rolls. They were chrysanthemums. Nice dark red ones, too.

"Look at these," I called. "Wonder how they got way out here."

Brains and Froth came over to me.

"Where were they?" Brains asked.

"Right here. By the side of the road."

"May I have them, please?" Froth asked.

I handed them over. Froth looked at them almost as carefully as he had the Rolls.

"Why, I say," Froth said. "This is most peculiar. Rather. These are the flowers I cut personally this morning for the vases in Madame's Rolls. There's a fine gold vase on each doorpost of the car. Someone has removed the flowers."

That didn't take much figuring out. But why? As I was trying to come up with an answer, Brains ducked into the rear seat of the Rolls. I saw him take the gold vases out of their holders. They were long, slender things. Brains handed one to Froth. He carefully inspected the other himself.

"These are the vases, all right," Froth said. "Although I must say, they *do* look a bit shinier."

"I don't think they are the same, Froth," Brains said. "Observe. Notice this grayish line. It's a slight scratch, yet it shows up remarkably against the golden shine."

Froth poked his face forward, his nose almost touching the vase Brains held.

"Is Mrs. Willoughby economizing these days?" Brains continued.

"Certainly not," Froth said indignantly.

"Then why does her magnificent car bear vases of cheap gold wash, applied, I believe, by the electroplating process?"

Froth began to rumble like an insulted volcano, but he couldn't get the words out.

Brains went on. "Scratch solid gold and the color revealed is still the color of gold, although somewhat less lustrous. Scratch a cheap wash and you reveal the base metal under it. The color of the scratch tells all."

"So what does it mean?" asked Dumb Bunny Carson.

"Someone," Brains said slowly, "is after something hidden in this car. They want it desperately."

He looked at me, and I could tell from the expression on his face that we were on to something big.

5 Hit-and-Run

The next day was Sunday. Dad and I walked down to the Sunny Spa—it's an ice-cream parlor and sells all kinds of stuff, including the Sunday papers. They always reserved a *Middlebury Herald* for us. We ran into Professor Benton and Brains there. They were getting their paper, too.

I didn't get a chance to talk to Brains, even though there were a thousand questions tumbling around in my head. The only conversation was a dramatic whisper Brains managed to shoot into my ear.

"The crime lab—within the hour. Important."

"Come along, Jimmy," my father called before I could even get in a whispered question in reply.

"Barclay, I'm ready to leave." That was Professor Benton, Brains' father.

So the Bentons left, walking north on Washington Avenue. The Carson family walked the other way, south.

When we got home, I kept asking my mother about dinner. We always had our big meal in the middle of the day on Sunday. I kept nagging her about how soon do we eat until my father took a hand.

"We will eat, young man," he said to me, "when your mother says it is time to. Not a minute before. Now, not another word out of you."

My father's tone of voice told me to go easy, or I'd never get over to the crime lab. My father is very strict about meals, especially about being on time for them. And, goodness knows, I'm late enough at times. So I could do nothing but wait until the roast beef was done. I didn't mind waiting for roast beef—my favorite meal. But it did seem to me that it took longer today than it ever had.

There were so many things puzzling me about yesterday's wandering car. I wanted them cleared up. Brains had some of the answers already. I knew that. Yesterday, after we had found the Rolls and Froth had driven it back, I had started firing some of my questions at Brains.

"Later, Operative Three," he had said. "We'll return to the crime lab, and I will explain."

I was getting pretty burned at Brains. Who'd he think he was, not answering any of my questions? I intended having it out with him when we got back to the crime lab, but when we got there, there was a message for me I couldn't ignore.

Mrs. Ray had met us.

"You are to go straight home, Jimmy Carson," she said. "Your father called."

Off I had gone. The rest of Saturday afternoon I'd spent mowing the lawn and helping Mom weed her flower beds and mulch them for winter. I couldn't get out after supper, either, even though Brains called twice. Dad had put a stop to that. He had simply said I was to stay home that night.

"You've been out every night this week," he'd said. "Try staying home once in a while. Find out what it's like."

Now, don't get me wrong. My dad's a swell person. He lets me get away with murder most of the time. Every once in a while, though, for no particular reason, he just puts his foot down. Oh, I try to wriggle out from under it, but Dad has a foot like an elephant. It puts down big and it puts down hard.

That's why I was so impatient for Sunday dinner. Mom finally called us. Dinner was finally over.

"Another piece of pie, Jimmy?" Mom asked. I was torn. Nobody makes apple pie like my mother does. But I wanted to get over to the crime lab.

"Later, Mom. I've got to meet Brains."

"Again?" my father harrumphed.

Gosh, I hoped he wasn't going to find something for me to do. He didn't. When my father gets behind the

Sunday paper, he's lost until he reads every word—even the ads.

I sped over to the crime lab as if my bike were jet-powered. I pressed the button on the secret panel and, in moments, was in the lab. Brains was waiting for me. He didn't say anything about my being late, but just glanced at his watch. That was his way of saying, "You're late."

"Strange things are happening, Operative Three," was his opening remark.

"And I foretell even stranger things to come," he continued.

"Sure, I know something mighty weird is going on, but what is it?" I asked.

"Before the sun sets this day we will be closer to the answer to the mystery."

We will?

"The pieces of the puzzle are beginning to fall into place."

They are?

"We must return to Mrs. Willoughby's. There is much to be learned at that estate."

Not again, I thought. *Not to see that cook.*

"Look, Operative X. Before we go, I've got some questions to ask."

"Proceed with your interrogation."

I banged out my questions.

"First off, explain to me how the Rolls got away from the Willoughby house without a driver."

"Later."

"And what's the meaning of those two quarts of sour cream?"

"Again, later. On our way to Mrs. Willoughby's. They are both pieces of the puzzle."

I hadn't done very well so far in getting answers, but with Jimmy Carson it's "if at first you don't succeed, keep hammering away."

"About those pieces. What are they, and how do they begin fitting?"

"Ah, Operative Three. Now you have asked an intelligent question." Brains paused, peaked his fingers, and leaned forward.

"It all starts with the letter from your Uncle Ed. Of that I am positive. As we began our investigation, we proceeded to the Willoughby estate. Separately, of course, but together in that we had a common point of interest."

This was going to take some time.

"Then, three things follow—all related. The Rolls is stolen. We learn that the sour cream consumption at the Willoughby household has increased suddenly. Next, what do we find? What is the next piece in our puzzle?"

He waited for me to answer. I waited for him to explain.

"We find the Rolls, abandoned. Your keen eyes— the eyes of a trained investigator—discover some discarded chrysanthemums. This leads us to an examination of the vases which had held those flowers only a few minutes before we found the Rolls."

"How do you know it was only a few minutes?"

"You're not thinking, Operative Three. Think back. How much time could have elapsed from the moment you saw the Rolls head down Toll House Road until you, Froth, and I found the abandoned car?"

"Couldn't have been more than, oh, I'd say about ten—maybe fifteen minutes."

"Precisely. So that gave the thieves only a short time to remove the original vases, from which they discarded the flowers, and replace the vases with the false ones. Remember, it took them some time to reach a point where they felt they could safely steal the vases and make their getaway unseen."

"Wait a minute, Operative X. Hold up. What do you mean, replace the original vases?"

"I thought I had made that perfectly obvious yesterday, Operative Three. Surely those so-called gold vases could never have been the original ones placed in a vehicle costing thousands of dollars."

"You mean that car was stolen just so somebody could snatch those vases?"

"Precisely."

"Then why didn't they just snatch the vases in the first place instead of taking the whole car?"

"Ah, you have again, as Froth would say, stroked the nail on the button."

Gee, guess I was better than I thought I was.

"I don't get it."

"The car was taken, true, with the immediate objective of obtaining those vases. But I feel quite sure the thieves wanted more time to search the car. The quick action on the part of you and Froth in pursuing the car prevented them from doing anything more than making off with the vases."

"Why the vases?"

"I can only assume, Operative Three, at this point, that whatever it is they are looking for resembles a vase."

"Oh," I ohed. "Why a vase?"

"That is the mystery. Once we know the significance of the vase-shaped object, then we will be nearing the heart of the matter."

I was beginning to get it.

"You see," Brains continued, "this case is like, and at the same time unlike, the problem we were confronted with in the case of the missing message. Then we knew what we were looking for, but didn't know where it was. In this case, we know *where* it is, but do not know *what* it is—yet."

I nodded my head.

"And we'll never find the answer here. Come."

"But what about the sour cream and the driverless car?"

"Later," Brains called over his shoulder as his head disappeared down the stairs. He was getting fond of that word.

We got on our bikes and headed east on Chestnut Drive toward Washington Avenue, heading out to the Willoughby estate. Just as we neared Tinker Drive, a short street that cuts straight through to Washington, we saw the white Rolls turn on to Tinker, also heading for Washington. It was moving slowly, almost as if it was waiting for something.

I sped up, calling to Brains, "Hey, that must be Froth. Let's catch up to him. Maybe he'll give us a ride out to Mrs. Willoughby's."

"And just how would we get back, Operative Three?" Brains asked. I didn't miss the note of sarcasm.

"Maybe he'd bring us back. Let's catch up with him, anyway. See, the light on Washington is changing to red. He'll have to stop. Hey, what's going on?"

The darndest thing was happening. Instead of slowing for the red light, the Rolls gathered speed. That wasn't like Froth. He was a very careful driver. Today, though, he ran through the red light. Just as he turned left, going against the light, a pedestrian stepped off the far curb. He stepped right smack in front of the oncoming Rolls. *Bang!* The Rolls' right front fender hit the man a glancing blow and sent him sprawling into the gutter.

The Rolls went on without stopping. It even speeded up.

Brains and I didn't speak. There were no cars coming at the moment, so we dashed across Washington and rushed to the side of the victim. We bent over him.

"Don't touch him," Brains ordered. "Don't try to move him. Can't tell how badly he's injured. Go phone the police."

I sprang up and dashed to an outdoor phone booth just across the street, digging in my pocket for a dime.

"Emergency! Police!" I shouted into the phone. "There's been an accident—a hit-and-run. Corner of Chestnut and Washington. Hurry! There's a man hurt!"

It seemed that I had just rejoined Brains when I heard the sirens screaming. Moments later a police car pulled up, followed by an ambulance.

We stood back as the white-clad intern made a quick examination of the victim. Then he signaled to the stretcher-bearers.

"Load him in," he ordered. "Doesn't appear to be too serious. But he may be in shock."

The ambulance pulled away, its sirens starting with a low growl, rising to a high-pitched scream.

"You boys see what happened?" the police officer said. It was our friend Officer McKeon.

"Yes, sir," we both answered, bobbing our heads.

"See the car?" Officer McKeon was all business. No friendly patter as we usually had with him. A hit-and-run accident is a serious matter.

"Yes, we did," Brains said.

"Get the license number? The make? The model?"

"Didn't need to," Brains said.

I put out a hand to stop Brains from going on.

"It was that white Rolls-Royce—Mrs. Willoughby's."

"Which way did it head?" Officer McKeon pressed his query.

"On up Washington."

"Thanks, Benton. That will be all for now. We may want to ask you both some questions later."

He strode away, climbed into the police car, and set off after the Rolls.

Brains looked at me. I looked at Brains. We both had the same thoughts in our minds.

We had informed on our friend Frothingham.

But what else could we do?

6 Frothingham Framed

As soon as the police car was out of sight, the crowd that had gathered pressed in on Brains and me and wanted to know what had happened.

Brains gave a very quick, brief description, not telling anyone in the crowd, though, that it was Mrs. Willoughby's car. Then he whispered to me, "Let's get out of here."

We got our bikes and headed north on Washington Avenue. We'd only gone a little way when Brains pulled over to the side of the road and stopped.

"Conference, Operative Three. We must talk this thing over."

"But don't you think we'd better get right on out to Mrs. Willoughby's? We've got to find out what in the world ever got into Froth. Why did he run through a red light? Why did he leave the scene of the accident, especially since he hit someone?"

"That's just it, Operative Three. Let's review what we have just seen."

Now, this was a twist. For once, I was the one who wanted to get out to Mrs. Willoughby's. Brains wanted to have a conference—a roadside conference. I wanted action; he wanted talk. We had talk.

"I think you're on to something, Operative Three," he started out. That made me feel pretty good. I didn't know just what I was on to, but if Brains said I was on to something, that was okay with me.

"You asked why Froth, a kindly man and a most careful driver, would ever run a light, hit a person, and then drive on."

"Beats me. Sure isn't like the Froth we've always known."

"Exactly. Now, did you see Froth driving that car?"

"Sure. Who else could it have been?"

"Think, Operative Three, think. He wasn't driving the car yesterday, was he—when it was roving?"

"No, but far as I know, nobody was."

"Oh, dismiss that idea of yours. I've told you I know what happened."

"Yes, you've told me *you* know. That makes just one of us."

"Yes, yes. But there's no time for that now. I repeat. Could you swear it was Froth driving just now? Think carefully, Operative Three. Much depends on this."

So I thought. I let the whole incident pass through my mind. Then I got what Brains was driving at.

"Hey, now that you mention it, I never did look at the driver of the car. I was so astonished to see Froth —I mean, who I thought must be Froth—run a red light, hit a guy, then drive on, that I guess I never did look at the driver."

"Exactly. I must admit that my reactions were much the same as yours. Neither of us could actually swear that we saw Froth at the wheel."

"That's right." I was thinking that Brains had it figured that if we had to go to court, neither one of us could testify *positively* that Froth was at the wheel.

But that wasn't what Brains had in mind at all.

"Someone else was driving that car, Operative Three."

"What!" I guess I must have howled in my astonishment at his statement.

"I'm positive of it. The accident was entirely out of keeping with Froth's character."

"You can say that again!" I said. Brains frowned at me. He hated that phrase.

"Now I ask you again to turn your mind back to the accident. The man who was hit by the Rolls. Did his actions seem to you to be in any way peculiar?"

I thought back again.

"Yikes! Now that you mention it, I remember at the time it happened it looked to me like the man deliberately stepped in front of the Rolls."

"Operative Three, allow me to congratulate you on your powers of observation. I had exactly the same idea."

This was really getting thick.

"Then, if that man just stepped right out in front of the Rolls. . . ."

"Frothingham was framed," Brains finished my sentence for me.

I could feel a slow burn of anger spreading through my veins.

"But can we prove it, Operative X? We're not sure whether Froth was driving, for one thing. And it's just our guess that the man deliberately stepped in front of the car. How are we going to prove his innocence?"

"By finding out, Operative Three, the motivation behind this strange series of incidents that have taken place in the last two days."

"Then you think this accident today is connected with what happened yesterday and also with Uncle Ed's letter."

"I'm positive of it, Operative Three. What we must look for is the missing link that connects these events."

"Creeps, if we only knew that."

"We will. We will. The firm of Benton and Carson has been challenged. We accept that challenge. We shall hurl it back!"

That suited me fine, but I still didn't know just in which direction I was supposed to start hurling. Brains answered that one.

"There was something else at that accident which I observed, but I doubt if you did. I mean—" Brains' tone suddenly became apologetic. He could see the resentment on my face. "I mean, you were telephoning the police when I noticed it."

"Go on."

"I must return to the crime lab immediately. But you go on out to Mrs. Willoughby's. Learn everything you can out there."

So that was it. Here my partner had been the one egging me on to visit Mrs. Willoughby's and the cook. But now, he's off to the crime lab, and I have to face that mad Kassabeban myself.

"If you have a chance to engage the cook in conversation, be sure and find out why he is using so much sour cream these days."

With that, Brains headed for the crime lab, leaving me at the side of the road with the icicles starting to form along my spine.

Carry on, Operative Three, I said to myself. A picture flashed through my head of Jimmy Carson all wrapped in grape leaves, stretched out on a big platter.

It took me about half an hour to reach the Willoughby estate.

I spotted the Rolls as I came around the last bend in the driveway. Right alongside it was the police squad car. The two cars sure looked funny standing there like that. There was the Rolls—a tall car, dignified, with classic lines—and next to it this squat police car with big tail fins and double red bull's-eye tail-lights, looking like a horned toad trying to strike up a conversation with a Great Dane.

Just as I was approaching the graveled circle in front of the garage, I spotted Froth's chauffeur cap. I stopped and popped it into my bike basket. Then I forgot to give it to Froth.

I didn't exactly forget to. It's just that by the time I pulled up alongside the Rolls, I saw that Froth was in no position to be interested in his chauffeur's cap.

Officer McKeon was talking to him.

"You'll have to come to the station with me, Frothingham."

"But, sir," Froth replied, "I repeat, I haven't been out of the house for two hours."

"But the Rolls was seen. We know it was Mrs. Willoughby's Rolls which hit the man and left the scene of the accident." McKeon turned to me. "This lad here saw the whole thing, didn't you, Jimmy?"

I gulped. Froth was looking right at me. I just nodded my head. Froth's face looked as sad as a basset hound's.

"Now, if you are innocent, Mr. Frothingham, believe me, you will be cleared," Officer McKeon said. "But for now, you will have to come to the station and be charged. Hit-and-run is a serious matter. No doubt Mrs. Willoughby will arrange bail for you."

"Bail! You mean I am to be imprisoned?" Froth reeled back, one hand on his forehead.

"Jimmy, Jimmy," he pleaded with me, "tell this officer I wasn't driving the car. If you saw the accident, you must have observed that it was not I at the wheel."

A backfire! Brains and I had just been figuring that since we didn't see who was at the wheel, we'd be able to help Froth. But now, since I *hadn't* seen the driver, I couldn't come to Froth's aid. I couldn't say *who* was at the wheel.

Froth waited for me to speak.

What a spot to be in!

"Gosh, Froth," I gulped, "I was so excited by the whole accident, the Rolls going through a red light and—"

"Hold it, Carson. You say the car went through a red light, too?" Officer McKeon had jumped on my remark.

I'd done it again—put my big foot into my big mouth.

"Yes, sir," I mumbled weakly.

Officer McKeon made another note in his book.

"Go on," he ordered. "Did you see this man at the wheel?"

"No, sir. That's what I was about to say. I was so excited by the whole accident that I don't think I even looked at the driver."

Creeps, had I cooked Froth's goose!

"All right, Frothingham. Let's go."

Frothingham cast me a sorrowful, how-could-you-do-this-to-me look as he walked over to the police car. He got in, and off they went.

I stood there. I had to fight back the tears. The last thing in the world I wanted to do was harm Froth, and look what I had done. I was so upset, I forgot all about seeing that crazy Kassabeban cook.

I got back on my bike and started pedaling slowly down the driveway, my head down, my eyes staring mistily at the ground passing below. What would I ever tell Brains? I had sure messed things up.

It was getting to be late afternoon. The setting sun was casting long shadows, making alternate strips of light and shadow on the asphalt drive. They flashed under my eyes. I was about halfway down the drive when it happened.

I heard a noise and looked up just in time to see a large rock the size of a basketball come rolling across the driveway, heading right for my front wheel. I cut sharply. The boulder just grazed my front tire. But my sharp cut was enough to send me flying over the handlebars. I hit that driveway with a dull thud. For a moment, I had trouble catching my breath. As I looked up, I saw a figure dart out from a clump of brush, partly hidden by a deep shadow.

He dashed over to my bike and grabbed the chauffeur's cap.

I leaped to my feet. I don't know exactly why. Guess I just figured if someone wanted that cap that badly, then I wanted it, too.

This figure—it was a man, his back toward me—started heading back into the woods. I nailed him with a beautiful tackle right at the edge of the road. I wish my coach could have seen that tackle!

The man crashed to the ground. I had him by the ankles. He lashed back with both feet and kicked me away. Then he leaped up and shot into the woods.

I got to my feet and started to follow him. *Hold up,* I told myself. *He's bigger than you are. This is no time to be a hero.* Then I saw the chauffeur's cap. The man, anxious to get away without being seen, had abandoned it. I guess it must have flipped out of his hands when I tackled him.

I picked up the cap and looked at it. I couldn't see anything unusual about it. The only thing I noticed was that the sweatband was sort of red-stained. *Red-stained!*

Blood!

Was it blood?

I got on my bike and headed back to Crestwood as fast as my legs could pedal me.

7 The Mug-a-Scope

It was dark by the time I got back to the crime lab. I'd have to hurry, because I knew that if I didn't report home shortly I'd be in trouble with my family. They didn't mind my being out at night, but they sure wanted to know where I was.

After Brains had pressed the right buttons and we'd given the sign and countersign, I hurried up the folding stairs and into the crime lab. I was bursting with my news, but before I could even get the second word out, Brains took the floor. He held it, too, despite my sputtering about how I had a lot to tell him.

"But first, Operative Three, I think I have made a discovery of major importance. I want your opinion. It is essential that you pay close attention, and give me your most carefully thought-out opinion."

Brains was working at his Mug-a-Scope.

"Observe, Operative Three."

He pressed a switch and his slide viewer lighted up. He took a round-shaped head—a silhouette he had cut out—and inserted it into the viewer. Then he glanced at me, his eyebrows raised in questioning half-circles.

"You can put your eyebrows back," I said. "You're not getting through to me."

Next he took two more cut-out pieces of black paper. They were identical. He fixed one of them on one side of the silhouetted face and one on the other, attaching them over the upper lip. You never saw such fancy mustachios.

"Please look again, Operative Three. Study this face I have reconstructed carefully. Take your time. Then I shall question you."

I looked and looked. I looked at that mock-up of a face close up. I moved back and looked at it from about ten feet away. A feeble flicker of light was beginning to illuminate my mind.

"Now, I ask you, Operative Three. Where have you seen such a face? Or perhaps I should ask, where have you had such a face described to you?"

Then it hit me. It was just the kind of face Uncle Ed had described in his letter—round, with big mustachios. It was the kind of face Uncle Ed said was Jujab's. He was the short, roly-poly man who had slipped out of Kassabeba with the tall drink of water called the Duke.

"It's Jujab, isn't it?"

A pleased expression came over Brain's face. He was the cat who ate the canary smothered in a pint of heavy cream.

"Exactly, Operative Three. Now, where have you seen that face within the past three hours?"

There he had me. I hadn't seen anyone with such big mustachios. I'd surely have remembered it if I had. I just shook my head.

"Do you recall, Operative Three, that when we had our roadside conference, I told you that I had observed something which I felt might have escaped your vigilant eye?"

I nodded my head. Brains was flattering and needling me in the same breath.

"The hit-and-run victim . . . you did see his face just before the police and ambulance arrived, did you not, Operative Three?"

"Sure, but if you think that man was Jujab, then where were his big drooping mustachios?"

"Ah, Operative Three. This is what I *observed* and you only *saw*."

"There's a difference between seeing and observing?" I demanded.

"Oh, but definitely. For example, you wear a wrist-watch, do you not?"

I nodded my head. He knew I wore a wristwatch.

"How many times a day do you look at it?"

I frowned. "Oh, twenty, maybe twenty-five times."

"Let's call it twenty times daily. Now, you've had that watch for a year plus eight months and two weeks. I recall you got it the Christmas before last."

Again I nodded my head.

"That would mean you have had it for a total of roughly six hundred and twenty days. Now, if you look at it twenty times a day, then you have looked at it twelve thousand four hundred times. You follow me?"

I guess I did, but I was dazed by all that multiplication he could do in his head.

"You've looked at it *twelve thousand four hundred* times. All right, now we'll see if you have *observed* as well as looked. Are the numerals indicating the hours on the face of the watch Arabic or Roman numerals?"

I racked my brains. "Arabic," I finally answered.

"If you will now observe," Brains said casually, "as well as look, you will find they are Roman."

I looked. He was right again.

"All right. You win. But what has that got to do with the hit-and-run victim?"

"I shall explain."

About time, too.

"When I was carefully inspecting the victim, I observed"—he stressed the word—"that the victim had covered his upper lip with suntan makeup. Why?"

He really didn't want an answer, so I didn't give any. That's not saying I had one.

"Because, obviously, this man had recently shaved off his moustache. Without the suntan makeup on his upper lip, the skin would have been most noticeable in contrast to the rest of his face, especially if it had been burned a deep tan by the Kassabeban sun."

"So it *was* Jujab—the hit-and-run victim?"

"I am positive of it. He would naturally shave off his moustache in an attempt to disguise himself."

"Then this just about proves Frothingham was framed. Hey! The driver of the Rolls must have been the Duke!"

"I feel certain of that, too, although we must have more actual proof. Surmise alone will not suffice." He looked over at the chauffeur's cap I had brought in with me. It was my turn to talk now.

I told him quickly about Froth's being carted off to jail, and my tussle with a stranger over the cap.

"And just look at this!" I was getting excited. "See the sweatband? It's all red, as if it might have blood on it."

Brains inspected it very carefully. "I don't think it is blood, Operative Three, although, of course, I shall subject the band to the proper chemical tests. But I feel sure this could be an important clue in our attempt to bring justice to Frothingham."

Just then Mrs. Ray buzzed the crime lab from the Benton house. Brains knew that was his signal to come in for supper, and I scooted on home.

The next morning I headed downtown to the *Crestwood Daily Ledger*. I checked with Brains first. He was going to be busy in the lab for the first two hours of the day. I was to come back after I'd seen Lew Jarman.

Lew Jarman is the star reporter on the *Ledger*. He's a real nice guy. He's only been out of college a year or two, but he's a real newshawk. I knew that if anyone could tell me just how bad the situation was for Frothingham, he could.

I was in luck. Lew was at his desk in the City Room —that's where the news stories are written and edited. Also, he'd been on late afternoon duty the day before. He calls it the dogwatch. That's because it's such a slow time. Only one man on—Lew, and he's there just in case any big story breaks, like a big fire, or some unusual police action.

"Hey, there, Jimmy Carson," Lew called as I entered the City Room. "How goes the firm of Benton and Carson, International Private Eyes?"

"We're on to something big, Lew," I replied.

With that, he sat up. He was all attention now, no longer leaning back lazily with his feet on the desk.

"What's it all about?" he asked. He reached for a pencil and a pad of copy paper.

"I don't think I've got enough information for you to take any notes yet," I said. "But this thing is building."

"And just what is this thing? I want the first story on it, Jimmy. Remember that."

He didn't have to worry about that. Lew was our friend. He'd always get a "scoop" if we could help him.

"Do you know anything about the case against Frothingham, Mrs. Willoughby's chauffeur?" I asked him.

"I covered the story myself," he answered. "It looks as if they've got him cold. Too bad. Froth's a nice guy. But running a red light, hitting a pedestrian, and leaving the scene of the accident—they're all serious charges, Jimmy. His alibi about being in the house alone at the time just won't hold. Officer McKeon tells me the car's radiator was still warm when he arrived at Mrs. Willoughby's. Now, what're you on to?"

"We think we know who *was* driving the Rolls when it hit that guy," I said, looking him in the eye. "And it wasn't Froth."

"*What?* Who?"

I hated to do it, but I just shook my head. I knew Brains would never forgive my spilling the beans about a case, even to a pal like Lew. I hoped Lew would understand.

He kind of half-smiled and leaned back in his chair again.

"Is Froth still in jail?" I asked.

"Oh, no. Mrs. Willoughby came down to the police station last night and put up bail. He's home now. But they took away his driver's license. He won't be piloting that white Rolls around for some time."

I gave this some thought. I mean about Froth's losing his driver's license. I had an idea. It was only a rough one, and I wanted my partner's opinion on it.

"Thanks a lot, Lew. I've got to go back to the crime lab now."

"Well, keep me filled in on this story," he said, grinning, "and tell your pal I'm all for both of you. If you need any help, count me in."

That was Lew Jarman for you. A real nice guy who knew that Benton and Carson were real operators.

When I got back to the crime lab, Brains had just finished running his tests on the hatband from the chauffeur's cap.

"No, Operative Three. It wasn't blood. It was some sort of red dye. Now, what did you learn from Lew Jarman?"

"Froth is out on bail. But he's lost his driver's license."

"That would be normal procedure."

"And I have a theory about the whole accident now."

"You have, Operative Three? I would be most interested in hearing it."

I shook my head. "Not until you clear up a couple of points. First, what's this theory of yours on how the Rolls roved with no driver?"

"Quite simple. Someone else was driving the Rolls."

"But I didn't see anyone at the wheel."

"You weren't meant to see the driver. You know how high the body of that Rolls is."

I surely did. The body of the car itself, just up to where the window glass begins, is almost five feet high. The body is like a big oblong box. It's some box, though. The Rolls is white and trimmed with solid gold. When I stand beside it, I can just see over the gold-trimmed windowsill and into the car.

"If a person driving that car wanted to remain out of sight," Brains continued, "all he would have to do would be to slump down. From the side of the road you were on, you wouldn't have seen him. He could keep his head low, peer through the steering wheel, but still have some vision through the windshield. Once he had passed you, of course, he could resume a more normal posture for his driving."

You see? I knew Brains would come up with a very simple answer.

"Does my explanation satisfy you, Operative Three?"

I just nodded my head. "How about that cream, though, those two quarts of sour cream?"

Brains leaned across his desk and picked up a thick book.

"I took this out of the library Saturday night." He held the book up. The title of it was *1,001 Nights of Exotic Near East Foods.*

"This cookbook," he went on, "lists the recipes for the dishes most favored in the Near East—Syria, Arabia, Armenia, Kassabeba, and so on. There is hardly a dish that does not require sour cream in large amounts. Usually the cream is that of goat's milk."

I shuddered.

"Now, the sudden increase in the consumption of sour cream at Mrs. Willoughby's has but one explanation. There has been an increase in those eating at, or about, the estate—particularly in those favoring foods from the Near East."

"The Duke and Jujab," I cut in.

"Right, Operative Three. And Khouri has been feeding them."

By now there was no doubt left in my mind that the two men Uncle Ed had written about were in Crestwood. We knew they were here. We knew they were after something hidden in the Rolls. We knew it was shaped like a small vase, but just what was it? And what was so important about finding it?

"Operative Three, we must proceed to the scene."

"What scene?"

"The estate of Mrs. T. Phillips Willoughby."

Oh, oh, I thought. *Here we go again.*

This time we really got an eyeful and an earful.

8 The Vanished Voice

When we arrived at Mrs. Willoughby's, we found a very sad Frothingham. He was in the garage, a chamois in hand, polishing the Rolls. He polished it every spare moment he had. It's a wonder he hadn't rubbed the paint off.

"Hello, James. Hello, Barclay," he said in a sorrowful tone of voice. "To think I may never drive this magnificent mechanism again." His voice was sort of choked up.

"Frothingham, I feel sure you will be back at the wheel of that Rolls before the week is over."

"You do?" Froth perked up.

"We are ready to place the full services of our organization at your disposal."

Froth looked puzzled.

"You have only to say the word," Brains continued.

"I say there, just what is this organization you speak of?"

Brains handed Froth our card.

The Benton and Carson
International Detective Agency

CONFIDENTIAL INVESTIGATORS AND CRIMINOLOGISTS
MODERN SCIENTIFIC METHODS AND DEVICES USED

| SHADOWING | FREE CONSULTATION |
| TRACING OF MISSING PERSONS | 24-HOUR SERVICE |

| *President:* | *Secretary-Treasurer:* |
| Barclay "Brains" Benton | James "Jimmy" Carson |

He studied the card. I could see Frothingham was impressed.

"You provide quite extensive services, I see. As a matter of fact, I do believe I have heard something of your activities in the past."

Brains bowed his head. "It is true that we have made our modest contributions to the solving of some extremely complicated mysteries," he said, bragging his head off. "It is the primary goal of the firm of Benton and Carson to see that justice is done. We firmly believe you have been framed."

"Framed? I'm afraid you'll have to explain, Barclay. I never shall get used to these American expressions."

"It means simply this: Someone deliberately caused that accident to throw suspicion on you—to put you in a most precarious position," Brains said.

"Oh, I see. But why would anyone want to do that?"

"Ah, that is the mystery. It's the first mystery we must solve. It is the key, I believe, to an even greater and more far-reaching mystery."

Then I remembered the theory *I* had about the reason for the accident. I'd meant to tell Brains about it on the way out. But his driverless car and sour cream explanations had made me forget my own ideas. I was just about to spout it when Brains took over again.

"Now, Froth, if we are to handle this case. . . ."

"Please do. Please do."

"Thank you for your trust in us. As I was saying, if we are to handle this case, then I must have a minute-to-minute report of your activities around the time of the accident."

Here I took over for a spell. "According to the *Ledger*, the police put the time of the accident at three-eighteen P.M., Sunday, September eighth."

"Good work," Brains said. "Now, then, Froth, suppose you account for your time from, say, three o'clock until the arrival here of Officer McKeon of the Crestwood Police Department."

Froth frowned. Then suddenly he beamed with joy.

"Ripping! Why didn't I remember to tell the police officer? I must have been terribly rattled. Simple. Really, most simple. I was taping a concert."

Brains looked at me. I looked back. Just what was Froth talking about?

"You see," Froth went on, "Madame is extraordinarily fond of Beethoven's First Piano Concerto, an infrequently performed work. It was being performed on a Sunday afternoon radio program. Madame, unfortunately, had to attend a meeting of the Garden Club. She would not be present to hear the concert so she requested me to tape it. This I did."

"Oh, I get it now. I mean, I think I do. You just plugged the tape recorder into the radio. Is that it?"

"Correct you are."

"But can't those things be preset? I mean, couldn't the police say, maybe, that you had the thing all hooked up and set to come on when the concert started?"

Froth smiled a little. "Many times in the past I've wished I could do just that, James, but unfortunately Madame's machine is incapable of being preset. I've even thought of buying some sort of timer for it, but I just never got around to it."

"So you had to be in the room while the machine was recording the concert yesterday afternoon," said Brains.

"Yes, Barclay. Had to—and most certainly was," Froth replied.

It looked to me as though we'd cleared Froth already. All he'd have to do was play that tape and the police would know he couldn't have been driving the

Rolls and recording the concert at the same time.

"Do you still have the tape, Froth?" I asked excitedly.

"But certainly."

"Then it's simple. We'll just play the tape for the police. . . ."

"One moment, please," Brains cut in. "Not so rapidly. It is true that Beethoven's First Piano Concerto is played infrequently, but not so infrequently that Froth couldn't have taped it before."

I didn't get it. What was Brains driving at?

"Unless we can definitely establish that Froth recorded that concerto *yesterday*, then the tape is of no value."

"But I can, Barclay," Froth cut in. "I always precede any taping with a few words, calling Madame's attention to some particular passage or phrasing. And furthermore, I always lead off the tape with the date of the concert and the orchestra or soloist who is performing."

"Excellent, Froth. Excellent. Let's play the tape and you'll be back at the wheel of the Rolls before nightfall."

We followed Froth into the house and into the music room. Froth went directly to a cabinet and took out a small round container.

"You see, right here on the cover. . . ."

We looked. Froth had typed a label: N.Y. PHILHARMONIC, SEPT. 8. BEETHOVEN'S FIRST PIANO CONCERTO.

"I shall play it for you. You will hear my voice speaking those words."

He threaded the tape into the machine and turned it on. We leaned forward.

Nothing.

Silence.

The reels were turning; that we could see. The only sound was the whir of the machine itself.

Froth, a puzzled look on his face, turned up the volume. Still no sound.

The tape had been erased.

9 A Lock of Hair

Froth snapped off the tape recorder. Gloom covered all of us like a collapsed tent. A long sigh whished out of Froth's mouth like air from a punctured tire.

The erased tape had erased his sudden hopes of being cleared of the accident charges.

"But how could it have happened?" Froth asked.

"Someone who knows that that tape could have cleared you deliberately erased the evidence. Has the tape been played since you recorded it?"

"Yes. This morning. Madame had her breakfast served in the music room just so she could hear it."

"Could anyone else have overheard it?"

"Only Harriet—the serving maid. Wait a minute. I do seem to remember the new chauffeur coming in for instructions once."

"New chauffeur!" Brains exclaimed.

"New chauffeur!" I squawked like a parrot.

"Why, yes. Madame considers herself most fortunate. She has always insisted on an English or continental chauffeur."

"And this new chauffeur? He's a foreigner?"

"Oh, no! He's an Englishman, like me," Froth said earnestly. "Or at least he claims to be. He does speak with somewhat of an English accent, although I thought I detected overtones of a middle-eastern accent in his voice, too."

Brains was leaning forward now, all ears.

"He appeared last night, just after Madame had procured my release from prison. He applied for the position of second chauffeur and, since his references seemed to be in order, he was engaged on the spot. It's extremely fortunate for Madame that he came when he did."

"It seems to me," Brains said, "that the new chauffeur's appearance at just the right time is so fortunate that it smacks of planning."

"I don't believe I follow you, m'boy," Froth said.

"Describe him, Froth," Brains directed, ignoring Froth's puzzled statement.

"Well, he's quite tall. Lanky, I believe, would be an American word that would fit him."

Tall and lanky! That's how Uncle Ed had described the Duke. My theory about the accident was looking better and better.

"Go on, Froth," Brains pressed on.

"Well, now, let me see. His face is quite long. He has a long, deucedly long, lower jaw, and—"

He didn't get any further, because just then Madame Willoughby came in. Maybe "zoomed in" is a better description.

"Boys, boys! Do remain seated. Oh, my poor, dear Froth . . . so much trouble . . . so sad . . . let me see you smile."

Froth smiled. It had about as much zing in it as a plate of wet noodles.

Mrs. Willoughby never stopped. "That's a good boy, Froth. Here, Barclay, James—you, too, Froth. Have some gumdrops . . . so good for quick energy . . . so good for troubled minds!"

She tossed back the feather neckpiece she wore most of the time. It was a long, dangly thing made of pink ostrich feathers. My sister Ann says it's called a "boa" —and it does look a little like the snake of the same name. Ann also says the boas must have been on Noah's Ark, so that will give you a rough idea of how Mrs. W. dresses.

Anyhow, she whipped out from under the feathers a fancy little bag on a string. It was made of tiny little beads sewn into a flower pattern. A long tassel, also made of beads, drooped from the end. As Mrs. Willoughby struggled with the drawstring at the top of the bag, the tassel caught in the boa and she wrestled with it the whole time she was digging into the bag.

Finally she made it. She held out a little paper bag of gumdrops to us.

"Go on, go on," she urged, "take several of them. I do so recommend the green ones . . . refreshing, very refreshing."

She sank down in an overstuffed armchair. "My, oh, my . . . so much trouble," she said again. "So many things to do, too . . . the police . . . Froth in jail . . . Froth out of jail . . . and the Prince . . . he's coming this after-noon, you know. He's such a dear boy. Trouble for him, too . . . his throne . . . they're trying to take it away from him. Oh, I do wish dear T. Phillips were still alive. He'd handle it all. Problems, problems. . . ." She paused, then came out with one word:

"Chrysanthemums!"

Now, how could anyone follow that rapid-fire con-versation? She'd covered a million subjects in one breath. I knew that "T. Phillips" was her late husband, but what else was she talking about?

"Chrysanthemums," she exclaimed again. "Must get some . . . you must cut some, dear Froth . . . right away . . . Fall Flower Show . . . Crestwood Chrysanthemum Club. . . ."

Frothingham bowed slightly. "Yes, Madame," he said and left.

"Oh, and the Prince will be here this afternoon," Mrs. Willoughby called after him. "I must meet him at the airport. Tell that new man, what's-his-name, will you?"

"Yes, Madame" came drifting back from the hall.

Brains kind of cleared his throat. "Is this Prince Halam you refer to, Mrs. Willoughby?"

"Oh, indeed, yes! He's coming here to enter Crestwood College . . . starts next week, doesn't it? I'm sure it does. But you'd know, Barclay, dear. . . . Professor Benton teaches there, doesn't he?"

Brains was starting to say "yes," and choking on the "Barclay, dear," both at the same time, when Mrs. Willoughby rose to her feet.

"I must tell Froth about the yellow pompons," she gasped. She swept out, having a return match with the feather boa all the way to the door.

I'd asked my father right after getting Uncle Ed's letter why the Prince had chosen Crestwood College. Oh, Crestwood's a fine school. It has a very good academic reputation among small colleges. But, after all, it wasn't Harvard, or M.I.T., or Stanford, or even State U. And I guess a prince could get into any of them if he wanted to.

Dad had explained it. T. Phillips Willoughby, Mrs. W.'s late husband, had grown up in Crestwood and had gone to Crestwood College. That's where he had met Mrs. W. After he had graduated, he went on to Cal Tech for a couple of years and took an engineering degree. Then he had gone to work for an oil exploration outfit. The job took him all over the world.

It was Mr. Willoughby who had discovered that Kassabeba was more heavily soaked with oil than a mechanic's coveralls. He had helped the old Emir, the Prince's father, to develop that small country into one of the richest oil countries in the world.

But Mr. Willoughby had never forgotten Crestwood College, or Crestwood, either, for that matter. After he had gotten rich, and I mean really rich, he had come back to Crestwood. He had built the Willoughby mansion for Mrs. W. and donated a dormitory to the college. It's called Willoughby Hall.

Every year, up until his death, Mr. and Mrs. Willoughby returned to Crestwood for a few weeks, usually in the fall. It's mighty pretty here in the fall. The leaves are all bright colors, and the weather is good.

Although Mrs. W. lived most of the time in Europe, she had continued her annual visits to Crestwood after her husband's death. She loved our little town, too. And in Europe she still had kept up a close friendship with the old Emir and looked on the Prince as sort of the son she never had herself.

That's why, my father said, the Prince decided to come to Crestwood College.

Suddenly, Mrs. Willoughby was back in the room. She headed for the armchair and was about to sink into it again when the new chauffeur appeared in the doorway.

"The car is ready, Madame. You requested it for eleven o'clock."

"Oh, yes . . . dear me! The Garden Club . . . I must fly, fly, fly! Here, dear boys, more gumdrops." She sprayed us with a handful and followed the new chauffeur out.

I knew Brains had looked the new chauffeur over as carefully as I had. He was built exactly as Uncle Ed had described the Duke. Tall, lanky, and horse-faced. One thing puzzled me, though. I couldn't imagine Uncle Ed forgetting to describe his most outstanding feature. That is, if this were the Duke.

The new chauffeur had the *reddest* hair I've ever seen on any head—even Brains'.

That fact, and that fact alone, knocked my accident theory in the head. Still, I thought I'd tell Brains about it.

We spent a few more minutes with Froth, trying to cheer him up. Then we headed back to town.

On the way, I explained my accident theory to Brains.

"I had it all figured out, Operative X," I said as we pedaled along. "About the accident, I mean. Until I saw the new chauffeur."

"Go on, Operative Three. I am most interested."

"Well, I figured it like this. That accident. . . ." I paused, collecting my thoughts. "I had it figured that accident was a real phony. Staged so Froth would lose his driver's license . . . am I making any sense so far?"

"But decidedly. Continue."

"Then the Duke, if it was the Duke doing the driving, could get Froth's job as chauffeur. That way he'd be right in the house. He could have plenty of time to search the car and keep an eye on Prince Halam, too."

"Exactly. My compliments, Operative Three. Your ratiocination has been of the highest caliber."

"My ratioci-*what*?"

"Your process of reasoning. It is most excellent. That is exactly what happened."

"You mean I'm right? Gee!" Boy, I felt pretty good. Then I remembered the one thing which tossed my theory into the ash can.

"But, Operative X. That couldn't have been the Duke. That screaming red hair . . . Uncle Ed would certainly have included that fact in his description."

"Have you never heard of hair dye, Operative Three?"

If I could have kicked myself without risking falling off my bike, I'd have done it. Hair dye! Of course!

"In this case, Operative Three, one of the villains removes hair from his face. The other changes the color of the hair on his head. Both are most effective methods of disguise. I am now more certain than ever that your uncle's Jujab and the Duke have insinuated themselves into the Willoughby household."

"You mean Jujab's there, too?"

"If I am not mistaken, we will find Jujab lurking very nearby. Perhaps in one of the garden houses which dot the Willoughby landscape."

"But he should still be in the hospital."

"A telephone call will ascertain whether or not he

has been released." We decided to check that out right away. We stopped to use the phone in Brains' front hall.

The call only took a minute.

Brains hung up and said, "The man who was hurt in the hit-and-run accident Sunday afternoon was discharged within an hour. He had only minor abrasions."

We crossed the Bentons' back lawn to the crime lab. Once we got upstairs, Brains went into one of his thinking spells. I could almost hear the bells ringing in his busy head.

"It's all falling into place, Operative Three," he finally said.

I didn't interrupt. I knew he'd go on.

"The Duke and Jujab are here. They have skillfully managed to insinuate themselves into the Willoughby household. Why? So they can have freedom of action to search the Rolls."

"For what?" I cut in.

"That's what we don't know as yet. And poor Froth is under a cloud. Charged with an accident which took place miles distant from where he was at the time. And now Prince Halam arrives."

Brains paused.

"Operative Three, we must work fast for two reasons. The coronation of the new Emir, the cruel Ras-Bey, is to take place, I believe, next Friday. That must be stopped. Also, we return to school next Monday. There is much to be done before then."

"Like what?" I wanted to know.

He looked at me carefully. I began getting that feeling I always got when Brains was about to hand me a really crazy assignment. I was right. This time he really handed me a beaut.

"At the earliest opportunity, Operative Three, I want you to get me a lock of the Duke's hair."

10 A Princely Story

Can you tie that?

All I had to do was get a lock of the Duke's hair!

When I asked him how I was supposed to go about handling this screwball assignment, Brains merely shrugged his shoulders.

"I have complete faith in your ingenuity, Operative Three." Some help!

I saw red all during my dreams that night. The next morning an emergency call from Brains sent me on my way to the crime lab. On the way over, I hoped Brains had changed his mind about the lock of hair. No such luck.

Brains was all excited.

"Prince Halam is here," he announced when I entered the inner sanctum.

This was the big news? This was the reason for the emergency call?

"Mrs. Willoughby told us yesterday he was arriving," I said.

"No, I don't mean that he's in Crestwood. He's right here in my house, talking to my father."

This *was* something.

"Mrs. Willoughby dropped him off this morning. Dad's taking him out to the college later on. But first I think we had better meet the rightful heir to the throne of Kassabeba. Come on."

Wow! I was getting excited. I'd never met a real live prince before. We knew he was coming, of course. Uncle Ed's letter had told us that. But to think that he was actually, at this very moment, in Brains' house —it was just like the movies.

As Brains and I were crossing the yard to his house I suddenly felt panicky.

"Brains," I said, stopping him, "how do you speak to a prince? I mean, what do you call him?"

"Your Highness, of course."

"You mean I've got to go in and say, 'How do you do, Your Highness?' 'Awfully glad to make your acquaintance, Your Highness,' and 'Are you enjoying your stay in Crestwood, Your Highness?'"

Brains didn't answer. He just sort of sniffed.

It was easy, though. Right off, I knew the Prince was going to be a swell person. He wasn't very big. Sort of slight, small shoulders, not much bigger than I am.

A little taller, but not any heavier. He had deep dark eyes and black hair. His skin was darker than ours, even with our summer tans.

What got me was that he was dressed just like any other college student. Gray flannel slacks, a sweater, and a sports jacket. I expected him to be dressed like those people you see pictures of attending the United Nations—you know, long white robes, maybe some sort of a nightcap on their heads. Not the Prince, though. He was dressed like any other freshman at Crestwood College.

When we entered Professor Benton's study, the Prince and Brains' father were looking over some papers on the desk.

"Why, good morning, James. Hello, Barclay. I want you boys to meet Prince Halam of Kassabeba. The Prince is going to be here with us at the college this year."

Brains did a deep waist bend and, with his head almost down to the floor, said, "This is a great honor, Your Highness."

I had started to step forward with my hand out for a handshake. I hesitated, then started to follow Brains' example.

The Prince stepped forward and put a stop to all that nonsense. He came around from behind the desk, held out his hand, and said, "Please just call me Halam. Forget that I'm a prince. I want to be treated like any other student at Crestwood."

Well, was I relieved! Brains had snapped up straight like a puppet on a string. When I looked at him, I could hardly hold back a laugh. Brains was actually blushing! He was embarrassed! *Serves him right*, I thought, *carrying on with that low-bow act*.

Professor Benton took over the conversation to keep us boys from being embarrassed any further.

"Halam and I were just going over his course of studies for his first year. I think we have his program well outlined by now. We were just about to leave for the college. Would you boys like to come along?"

Would we!

Crestwood College is located northeast of the town. We drove up to Channing Street, turned right one block to Poplar, then left again to College Road.

Professor Benton took us all around the campus. It's really something to see this time of the year. The grass is all green. The old trees haven't started shedding their leaves yet, although they've begun to change color, showing yellow and red against the green.

Prince Halam was only slightly interested in the football stadium. It's a small one, but you can really see a football game in it. You're not miles away from the playing field as you are at State U.'s great big one. When Brains' father told Halam that they also played soccer games in the stadium, the Prince picked up interest. It seems soccer is a big thing in Europe. I've seen a couple of soccer games, and it's okay, but give me football every time.

After we'd toured the campus, we went to Professor Benton's office. Brains hadn't said much, but he was fidgeting, I could tell. Brains was just about to burst, he had so many questions he wanted to ask. Once we were all seated, the professor behind his desk, the rest of us sort of sprawled in big, leather-covered chairs, Brains asked a leading question, and Prince Halam took over.

"Oh, yes, Barclay," he said, "things are quite different in my country. Our food, our customs, our clothes."

"Call me Brains," Brains cut in. "Everybody does—except my parents."

Professor Benton looked at Brains and smiled.

"All right—or, rather, okay, Brains. Is there anything you would like me to tell you about in particular?"

"Yes. I should like very much to hear about the coronation. I know it should be you who is being crowned. Jimmy's Uncle Ed wrote us all about it."

A sad expression crossed the young Prince's face. He shook his head as if to toss such thoughts away. Then he smiled.

"Your Uncle Ed is a very fine man, Jimmy," he said to me. "I've flown with him many times. He even let me take the controls once in a while. That was in England. I haven't been back to Kassabeba since your uncle became my father's pilot."

"The coronation is this coming Friday, isn't it, Halam?" Brains asked.

"Yes. I fear it will come off as scheduled. I know those loyal to me have done all in their power to uncover the plot of my half uncle, Ras-Bey, to seize the throne. But . . . well, perhaps someday I shall be able to go back to my people."

"What goes on at the coronation?"

"Oh, it's a wonderfully colorful affair. Of course, I've never seen one—only pictures of one, my father's. You see, he ascended the throne many, many years before I was born. Had he reigned two more years, he would have ruled longer than any other Emir in the history of my country—fifty years. He was a good man. The money from the oil fields developed by Mr. Willoughby was wisely spent to improve living standards among the poor. Ras-Bey will change all that."

Halam's voice became bitter when he mentioned Ras-Bey.

"Now that my country is so rich in its oil deposits, the coronation will be attended by representatives of all the European powers. There will be chieftains from Africa, sheikhs from the Near East, rajahs from India, and England, of course, will be represented. Kassabeba was once a British protectorate. Even your country, the United States, will send a delegation, since it was your country and one of its citizens, Mr. Willoughby, who did so much to advance Kassabeba.

"The coronation ceremony lasts almost the full day," the Prince continued. "Tribesmen from the desert ride in on their horses and race through the streets around the palace. There is a military parade. This time, our air force—only four planes—will fly overhead. But the high point of the ceremonies comes at the end of the day."

Now I could see Brains was all attention. He leaned forward. His ears seemed to swing out from his head and rotate like radar antennas.

"That's when the ascending Emir must sip the Pure Water of Life with the poorest beggar in the land."

"How is this beggar selected?" Brains wanted to know. I wanted to know what the "Pure Water of Life" was, but I kept still.

"In the case of Ras-Bey, I'm sure it is one of his relatives. The beggar, you see, is endowed with enough riches to enable him to live in ease and comfort the rest of his life. Often, he becomes an official in the new Emir's court. I know when my father was crowned, that was what happened."

I decided to say something.

"What's this 'Water of Life'? And why doesn't the Emir just drink it himself?" I wanted to know.

"It's a symbolic ceremony. The water comes from a pure crystal spring high in the mountains. The Emir sips it to show his humility. He sips out of the same vial with the lowliest person in the country. That is to show that he is one of the people. It shows that he is as much a subject to their wishes as they are to his."

"This vial you mentioned," Brains cut in. "What's it like?"

"It is made of gold, and encrusted with jewels entwined with small golden leaves. It is not much larger than a rose vase."

At the mention of the word "vase," Brains shot a look at me. I started to say something, but Brains shook his head at me. I closed my mouth.

"This vial has been handed down from one Emir to another for many generations. It is kept closely guarded in the palace. I've never seen it. Only a picture of it. If I had the vial, then I would be the one ascending the throne next Friday instead of Ras-Bey."

"You mean, unless you have the Golden Vial, you cannot be crowned?" Brains wanted to know.

"That's right, Brains."

With that remark, Brains pulled in his antennas. I knew his mind was working at high speed. Finally he came up with another question.

"What year and month was the coronation held for your father?"

"The time was our season of the Golden Cheese. You would call it August. The year was 1912."

Brains just sat there nodding his head, looking wiser than any owl.

Professor Benton spoke up.

"I think you boys had better run along now. Prince Halam and I still have one or two matters to straighten out in his program."

We left. Outside, Brains strode along the campus, head down, his skinny knees cutting the air like scissors. I almost had to trot to keep up with him. Brains kept looking at his watch.

"The buses to Middlebury leave every hour. On the hour," he said aloud but more to himself than to me.

"That's right," I said, although he hadn't really asked me. "Why? We going to Middlebury today?"

"Immediately. I believe if I hurry, I can catch the next bus."

"Sure, we can make it easily. We've got almost twenty-five minutes to get to the bus station."

"You, Operative Three, are not going."

"I'm not! Why?"

"I am going to Middlebury on a mission of research. A mission that I can handle alone. There are important things for you to do here."

I groaned to myself. I knew even before he said it what one of the important things was.

"The hair from the head of the Duke is becoming more and more important. I shall want it on my return."

"I'm not a barber," I said, kicking at a big horse chestnut. I wanted to go to Middlebury, too.

All the way back to the Bentons' house I kept asking and asking, "How'm I going to get this chunk of hair?" Operative X said absolutely zero.

Back at the crime lab, Brains got his bike and headed for the bus station. I got mine and headed back to Mrs. Willoughby's and an adventure I was lucky to get out of alive.

11 The Daring Dangle

So Brains was off to Middlebury without me, his partner, Operative Three. I didn't know what he was going to do there, but I sure did know that whatever it was I'd gladly trade places with him.

Brains had been mighty secretive in the last two days. He wasn't telling me all he knew. I didn't like that, but I did know that Brains always acted that way when he was nearing the solution of a mystery. He liked to have everything all wrapped up nicely and neat as a box of candy before he started handing out solutions.

I turned off Toll House Road into the Willoughby driveway. I kept my eyes wide open for bouncing boulders. When I got to the bend just before you reach the circle in front of the garage, I hopped off my bike and hid it behind a clump of bushes.

I crept up quietly. I wanted to see what might be going on. I poked my head from behind a bush just in time to see something that really set me back with surprise.

It was Jujab, the hit-and-run victim. If he had been hurt, even a little bit, he sure didn't show it now. He came around from behind the garage on the double and bounced up the outside stairs leading to the chauffeur's apartment as spry as an antelope—if you can imagine a ball-shaped antelope.

I pulled back into my hiding place in the big bush and waited. I didn't have long to wait. Jujab came out, followed by the Duke. They came down the stairs and walked to the front of the garage. The doors were open and I could see the Rolls inside. For a moment they talked to each other. Their voices were so low I couldn't make out what they were saying. Then Jujab nodded his head, and both men took off down the path leading from the back of the garage to a garden house about a football-field length away.

I waited until I could just see the tops of their heads in the distance. This was my chance. Now or never. I sprinted across the circle and dashed up the stairs. Lucky for me, the door to the apartment was open. I shot through it and started looking around.

In the bedroom I found what I was after. On the bureau was a hairbrush. In the hairbrush were four red hairs. Not a lock, like Brains said he wanted. But four hairs were better than none. I pulled them carefully out of the brush and wrapped them in a piece of Kleenex.

I felt pretty good. The whole thing had gone a lot easier than I expected.

I headed for the door. Just as I got there, I heard voices. Jujab and the Duke were coming back. They weren't more than fifty feet away. I couldn't possibly get down those stairs without their seeing me. I pulled back, looking for a place to hide. If they came up to the apartment I was a goner.

Creeps! Did I ever heave out a sigh of relief when they went right by the foot of the stairs and into the garage. It took me a few minutes to realize I wasn't much better off now than I had been before. I still couldn't get out of the apartment until they left.

I noticed a vent on one side of the living room. I moved over to it, walking on tiptoes. I didn't want those two down below to hear any noises coming from above them. The vent was open, and I could hear the Duke and Jujab talking. They still kept their voices low, although I could catch a word or two every now and then. One word I made out was "quarry." Then I heard a whole sentence, clear as could be. My spine turned into a piece of cooked spaghetti.

"I'll go upstairs and get it," I heard the Duke say.

I don't know what "it" was. I just wanted to make sure it wasn't going to be me. I had to find a place to hide. I could hear the Duke coming up the stairs.

Creeps! I wished there were a million of them. He was about halfway up and my heart was halfway down, headed toward my shoes.

"I say there, old chap!"

The footsteps climbing the stairs stopped.

"What is it?" I heard the Duke reply.

The voice calling the Duke was Froth's. Good old Froth!

"Madame wants to see you. Immediately."

"All right, all right," the Duke called back. He didn't sound very happy about the summons.

I could hear him going back downstairs. I waited until I thought the coast was clear. Then I slipped out the door and down those steps three at a time. I ran around the back of the garage and pressed my body to the rear wall. I waited. There was a window only a few feet away. I got down on my hands and knees and crept over until I was directly underneath it. I slowly raised my head, just in time to see the Duke come back into the garage. Jujab was waiting for him. Now I could hear them plainly.

"Her Ladyship wants the car in an hour," the Duke said with a sneer. "We'll have to hurry."

With that, the Duke climbed into the Rolls and Jujab got in beside him. The Duke backed the Rolls out, turned it around, and headed down the driveway.

I sprinted around front. Froth was standing there.

"Come on, Froth," I hollered. "We've got to follow them."

Froth didn't hesitate. He hopped on Mrs. Willough-by's bike and went whizzing down the driveway just as I retrieved my bike and joined in the pursuit.

At Toll House Road, Froth halted.

"Perhaps you will now tell me where we're going and why?"

"Don't know why, Froth, but I think I know where. Come on."

We pedaled about a half mile down Toll House Road. Then I turned left into a narrow dirt road. Froth was right behind me. No questions asked. He followed where I led.

I was pretty sure I knew where the Duke and Jujab were going. I'd heard the word "quarry," and that could only mean Turner's rock quarry. It was the only quarry around. It's abandoned now, has been for several years. I still didn't know why the Duke and Jujab would want to take the Rolls there, but I was going to find out.

As we neared the quarry, I signaled for a halt. We pushed our bikes off the road and proceeded very cautiously on foot.

There was a narrow entrance to the quarry. When it was being worked, the trucks hauling the stone made their turnarounds down in the quarry. It was about as big as three tennis courts put side by side. It went down deep, forming a large hole with the sides going straight up. One side sort of hung over, like a lip. When we reached the entrance to the quarry, we saw

the Rolls. It had been pulled under this overhanging lip, sort of in a pocket with the rear of the car almost up against the bank.

Froth and I crept up along the edge of the quarry until we reached the lip. We crawled out on it. I held my breath, hoping it wouldn't give way.

We lay there, stretched out on our stomachs, our heads just poking over the edge. The top of the Rolls was about ten feet below us.

"Can you see what they're doing?" Froth whispered.

"I can just see the top of the Duke's head," I whispered back, craning my neck for a better look. "He's opening the trunk, I think."

"The trunk? What trunk?"

Then I remembered. "What you call the boot."

In a moment the Duke came around to the front of the car near the driver's seat.

"He's got a small black box in his hand. Looks like it has a dial on the top of it," I reported to Froth.

The Duke got into the car and Jujab followed. I couldn't see them anymore. Couldn't hear what they were saying, either. I had to see what was going on. I wanted to know what they were looking for. I wanted to see *where* they were looking. I inched back and touched Froth on the shoulder.

"Froth, I've got a plan. I'll need your help, though."

"Anything you say, m'boy."

When I think back, I must have been out of my mind to dream up my idea. My brains must have been bunched in the top of my noggin from looking down so long. Anyway, I did it.

"I've got to see inside that car, Froth."

"But how, m'boy? How?"

I looked at Froth's long arms. I'm over five feet tall. My height plus Froth's arm length, and I thought I could do it.

"It's like this, Froth," I whispered and then outlined my plan. Froth didn't think much of it, but he went along with me.

That's why, about three minutes later, I was hanging head down, my hands touching the roof of the Rolls, with Froth hanging on to my ankles. I was dangling over the side of that quarry, upside down like a circus acrobat.

Slowly I let my head come closer to the roof of the Rolls, letting the weight of my body rest on my arms. I heard Froth give a grunt once. I flashed a mental message to him: *Hang on, for Mrs. Carson's sake!*

Very slowly I pushed my body out until my head was directly over the rear window of the Rolls. Again I started lowering myself down.

Now my eyes were level with the top of the rear door. I hoped Froth could stretch his arms another couple of inches. He could. I went down until my eyes were peeking into the car just at the top of the window.

There were the Duke and Jujab. Lucky for me, their backs were turned toward me. The Duke had this black box in his hands and was rubbing it back and forth over the upholstery in the rear seat. Jujab had one hand cupped behind his left ear, his head twisted into a position of acute listening.

What were they doing? What was that black box? I never found out. Not then, I mean. Jujab turned around, and his fat, round face showed up right by my window like a moon. His black, beady eyes were staring right into mine. I don't know who was the more astonished or frightened. Must have been some scare for him, though, to see an upside-down face hanging outside the car window.

"Eeeeeeeowwwww!" Jujab howled.

"Pull me up!" I yelled.

Froth lost his grip on my ankles, and I went tumbling down. I landed between the car and the side of the quarry. The breath was knocked out of me for a moment. I heard the car doors slam and knew the Duke and Jujab were after me. I jumped up.

The Duke and Jujab moved in. I was crouched right by the trunk of the car, my hand resting on it. I felt my hand close over the car keys which were dangling from the trunk lock. Without thinking, I pulled them out.

The Duke and Jujab came at me, one from either side. I looked up. I could see Froth's face hanging over the quarry's edge. His eyes were big as saucers.

The Duke and Jujab sprang. In the same instant, I leaped straight up, resting my hands on the Rolls' shiny white "boot" and pulling my legs up after me as quickly as I could. Out of the corner of my eye, I saw the Duke and Jujab meet like a couple of runaway express trains, Jujab's round skull taking the Duke right in the midsection. The grunts they gave out with were music to my ears.

As they started to untangle themselves, I slid down the side of the Rolls and made a dash for the quarry entrance. I hoped for Froth's sake that I hadn't scratched off any of that precious paint when I slid off the car, but I didn't have time to worry much right then. The Duke and Jujab began yelling. In a second, I heard their footsteps pounding after me. I poured on the coal. They were gaining on me fast, but as I reached the entrance, I twisted around for a quick look. Just as I turned, the Duke, who was in the lead, snagged one of those long, skinny legs of his on a rock and went sprawling. Jujab bowled into his fallen partner and did a complete somersault before skidding to a stop in a cloud of dust.

I broke the world's record for jumping on a bicycle.

When I looked back again, I saw that Froth had made it down from the rim of the quarry and was pedaling like mad up the road after me. Then I noticed I still had the keys to the Rolls in my hand. I started laughing. I couldn't hold back. Froth came alongside and looked at me as if I were nutty as a fruitcake.

"I fail to see any hilarity in the present situation," he panted.

I held up the keys, dangling them in front of his face.

"These keys—they're the keys to the Rolls. The Duke and Jujab are stuck. They can't get back."

With this, Froth frowned.

"But they must," he said. "We must return the keys."

"What!" I howled. "Go back there and hand over these keys?"

Froth nodded his head solemnly.

"Madame needs the car within the hour."

12 The Silver Ghost

"You returned the keys?" Brains asked.

"Me! Creeps! I should say I didn't. I wouldn't have gone back to that rock quarry for anything."

"Then I presume Froth did."

"You presume correctly. Where Madame is concerned, Froth's more loyal than an Eagle Scout."

We were back together in the crime lab. After I had given the keys to Froth, I had scooted away from the quarry like a scared rabbit. I'd like to have seen Froth present those keys. He probably went back there and handed them over as cool as a cucumber with a remark something like "You were looking for these?"

"In the excitement of your adventure, I trust you carried out the mission which was your primary reason for visiting Mrs. Willoughby's," Brains said.

Creeps! I'd forgotten all about the red hairs. My hand shot to my hip pocket. I hoped they hadn't fallen out when I was dangling upside down. My hand felt the Kleenex. I sighed with relief and pulled the package out. I opened it and held it out to Brains, palm upward.

Brains picked up the four hairs. He looked at them closely.

"Excellent, Operative Three. My congratulations."

"Well, thanks, Operative X. I'd like to know, though, just what those red hairs have to do with this Kassabeban caper."

"You must recall, Operative Three, that we have two mysteries on our hands. Two cases to solve. One concerns the false hit-and-run charge against Frothingham; the other, what are the Duke and Jujab looking for in the Rolls?"

"And what are they looking for?" I asked.

"I think I know now. I shall make it even stronger. I'm almost positive that I know. That was the reason for my trip today to Middlebury."

Brains paused, and his forehead wrinkled up in deep thought. "It's strange, though," he said. "When the Prince was telling us about the coronation ceremony, he left something out. He didn't mention a very important part of the ceremony. Perhaps it merely slipped his mind at the moment, but—" Brains paused again— "but I think it much more likely that he himself may not know about this integral part of the ceremony."

"Then you found out even more than you were looking for?"

Brains nodded his head. "State U. has a magnificent library. They have microfilms of the world's outstanding newspapers, dating back to the turn of the century. The *New York Times*, the *Manchester Guardian*, and, of course, the London *Times*."

I didn't get the "of course" part, but I let Brains go on.

"I should like to inquire of Frothingham or Prince Halam about the history of that Rolls. Do you suppose we could see Froth tonight?"

I was anxious to see if Froth was okay. I mean, I hoped he hadn't had any trouble with the Duke and Jujab when he handed them back the keys to the Rolls. I said, "Sure."

A telephone call solved our problem.

Professor Benton called from the house. The Prince was with him. They had just come back from the college, and Professor Benton thought we might like to go along when he took the Prince back to Mrs. Willoughby's. The Prince was staying with her until school started.

There were lots of questions I wanted to ask Brains, but I couldn't very well in front of his father and the Prince. Brains hadn't said so, but I felt pretty certain that what we were looking for was a vase-shaped object. Could it be the Golden Vial? That didn't seem possible to me. Wouldn't it still be in Kassabeba? It was a very important part of the coronation ceremony —the *most* important part. It couldn't have gotten out of Kassabeba. That's what I thought. Maybe Brains had different ideas.

He did.

When we reached Mrs. Willoughby's, there was Froth, leaning on the white Rolls again, still wearing his basset-hound expression. At least there were no physical marks on him to show he'd had any trouble with the Duke and Jujab.

Professor Benton went into the house to say hello to Mrs. Willoughby. The Prince stayed outside while we talked to Froth.

"Do you know anything of the history of this Rolls, Froth?" Brains asked.

"Why, yes. It's one of the last Silver Ghosts made."

"Silver Ghost?" I asked.

"That was what the makers named this particular model. The last ones were made in 1925."

"You mean this car is—"

"More than twice as old as you are."

It surely was.

"This particular Silver Ghost was built to definite specifications for Prince Halam's father. Long before His Highness was born, of course. Do you remember the car, Prince Halam?"

"Not very well. I do know that years ago, it had a platform jutting out from the rear. My father's body-guards rode on it, standing up. You see, before we became as democratic as we are now in my country, no servant could ride in the same enclosure with the Emir."

What a picture. This great big old Rolls, all white, trimmed with solid gold, rolling through the desert with two bodyguards in flowing white robes hanging on for dear life behind.

"How did Mrs. Willoughby acquire the car?" Brains asked. "Has she had it long?"

"No, not long . . . about six or seven months. It was left to her by the Emir. She had always admired the car, and it was understood that on his death the car was to be shipped to her in England.

"I remember when it came over," Halam said. "I was at Eton. Froth drove her down to school. Then, when she came to America, she wouldn't dream of leaving the car behind."

Brains was thinking.

"Why are you so interested in the car's history, Barclay?" Froth asked.

"I'm positive that this car holds the key to Prince Halam's future."

"The key?" We all asked at once.

"What I refer to is a vase-shaped object that I am firmly convinced is secreted somewhere in this magnificent machine."

I remembered back to earlier in the day and my scary experience at the rock quarry.

"I guess the Duke and Jujab must think so, too.

They were sure giving that Rolls a going-over with that black box," I said.

"With *what?*" Brains demanded.

"A black box. Didn't I tell you about it?"

"Would I be asking you if you had?"

I guess he wouldn't. I felt a little shamefaced at forgetting about it.

"They had this black box. It had a dial on it. They were rubbing it all over the upholstery."

"A Geiger counter!" Brains said, all excited.

Looking for uranium in a Rolls? I asked myself. *Oh, come on, Brains!*

I was just about to ask him what color padding he wanted in his cell, when he said, "Froth, Prince, Jimmy—we've got to kidnap that Rolls!"

13 Catwalk and Mice

Now, just how did Brains think we were going to kidnap the Rolls?

I didn't have a driver's license. Neither did Brains. We weren't old enough. Froth's license had been lifted by the police. Prince Halam had a British license, but we didn't know whether it would be good in the United States. And Halam didn't want to take any chances. I didn't blame him.

"Why do we have to take the car?" I asked Brains.

"To search it. To go over it inch by inch, part by part."

"But that's what the Duke and Jujab have been doing. If they haven't been able to find whatever it is we're going to be looking for, what makes you think we can?"

Brains frowned at me.

"The firm of Benton and Carson never says die. We succeed where others fail," he said.

"Couldn't we just do our searching here? After all, it's Mrs. Willoughby's car. If it's all right with her...."

"And if we find the object, wouldn't the Duke and Jujab know we had found it? Wouldn't they go to desperate lengths to get it from us? No, we must search this car at a spot far from the Duke and Jujab."

How to get the Rolls to that far-removed spot was the big problem. It wasn't going to be settled that night, though. Professor Benton came out of the house, and we had to go.

I had a lot of chores to do around the house the next morning, so Brains had to stew over the problem of how to get that Rolls away all by himself.

About eleven o'clock, my mother came out on our back porch. I could tell she was all excited. I was stacking some logs for our fireplace.

"Jimmy! Jimmy!" she called. "Come in. Hurry up. Your Uncle Ed is on the telephone."

Uncle Ed? Calling me? All the way from Kassabeba? This must be something big. I ran into the house. My mother was already back on the phone, chatting with her brother.

"Here he is, Ed."

"Hi, there, young man. How's every little thing?"

Gosh, his voice was just as clear as if he were calling from Bleeker City, three miles away.

"Are you calling all the way from Kassabeba?"

I heard him laugh. "Nope, Jimmy, I'm calling you from Langston. I'm at the Strato-Air plant. Just hopped over from Kassabeba to pick up a new plane. She's a pure jet, and a sweet job she is, too. I thought you and Brains might like to come down here and look her over. How about it?"

"Gee, swell, Uncle Ed."

"Okay, then. I've already cleared it with your mother. Why don't you and Brains hop the first bus you can get and come on down? I'll rent a car and bring you back. I think I'll be able to stay around for two or three days. There are several things I want to check out on this new jet job, so when you get here, come to Hangar Ten. That's where the plane is. I'll be around there somewhere. Okay, Jimmy?"

"You bet!" I shouted back.

"Okay, then. Be seeing you. 'Bye."

"Good-bye, Uncle Ed."

"It's okay, Mom?"

"Surely, Jimmy. Now, you change into your good clothes. I'll make some sandwiches for you to eat on the bus. Better call Brains right away and see if he can go, too."

I was back on that phone in a flash. Brains took the news of Uncle Ed's appearance as if it were nothing for a person to suddenly drop in from halfway around the world. But I could tell he was just trying to cover up his excitement. He wanted to see that plane and

Uncle Ed just as much as I did.

"Have you ascertained at what hour the next bus leaves for Langston?" he asked.

I could have exploded. Did I have to do all the work?

"Look, Operative X," I said, "I've got to call Stinky Greene and see if he can do my paper route. How about your making that call?"

"As you say, Operative Three."

"Then come right over as soon as you find out."

My answer was the sound of Brains' telephone being replaced in its cradle.

Stinky said he could do my paper route. Mom made the sandwiches. I waited. Seemed to me I waited and waited and waited. I also fumed. No Brains. It got to be one o'clock. Still no Brains. I was getting worried. Had something happened? Had Brains suddenly thought of something more important? And if he had, why hadn't he called me?

I went out on our front porch, plenty burned. I cooled off when I saw my partner come pedaling slowly up the street.

"What took you so long?" I asked, and if my voice sounded sort of cross, that's exactly how I wanted it to sound.

"Why, Operative Three! There's no hurry. The bus doesn't leave for Langston until two o'clock."

After what seemed like a week, two o'clock, and the bus, came.

Langston is southwest of Crestwood, about a

hundred miles away. The bus trip takes nearly three hours, since it's a local run, with the bus stopping at every wide place in the road between Crestwood and Langston.

The Strato-Air Aircraft Company had located in Langston only three years ago. Gee, you never saw such activity as when they moved in. They picked Langston because the country around there is flat, with plenty of room to lay out airstrips long enough to handle jets. The company makes jet bombers for the Air Force and passenger airliners—great big planes that can carry a hundred and twenty passengers.

That town of Langston had really mushroomed. A whole new city sprang up overnight. Strato-Air employs over twelve thousand men and women.

Brains and I had been there two or three times—our parents took us down just to see the place—so when we reached Langston, we knew where to go. It's all Strato-Air, though, so we couldn't have gone too far wrong no matter what.

It was beginning to get dark when we reached the gates of the plant. The guard on duty checked us out very carefully. It was a good thing Uncle Ed had left our names with him. You can't just wander into Strato-Air. They have security guards all over the place. That's because those new jet bombers for the Air Force are top secret as to their speed, performance, and bombload.

This guard looked us up and down and sideways.

Finally he called another guard who came to the gate in a jeep, and he took us over to Hangar Ten.

What a hangar! I bet it covered ten acres. It had a high, arched roof made of glass, the floor was cement, and everywhere you looked you saw small tractors and motor scooters for the mechanics to use getting from one end to the other in a hurry. The hangar was that big and long.

Catwalks ran at crazy angles all over the place. There were retractable ladders on small trucks. Those jets are pretty high. Working on the top of one or on the tail assembly, you're more than thirty feet off the ground.

We looked around.

"Kind of gloomy in here," I said to Brains. It was getting dark fast and the light coming through the glass roof was spooky.

There wasn't much activity. I guess they only worked one shift in this hangar, but we had seen the shifts changing in other sections of what they call the Strato-Air Complex as we jeeped over to the hangar.

There was no sign of Uncle Ed.

"Let's see if we can find the plane," Brains suggested.

We walked toward the center of the hangar, passing silvery planes, big, silent, and ghostly. I thought it was strange that we didn't meet any workers, but it was after five o'clock. I figured Uncle Ed was probably in the plane, checking it or something.

"There she is," Brains whispered, pointing to a plane up ahead of us. He had taken hold of my arm.

"Yes. That's it, all right." I found myself whispering, too, although I didn't know why.

There were aluminum ladders angled against the wings of the aircraft. There was one of those motorized ladders against the tail assembly. Running the length of the plane there was a suspended catwalk.

The retractable loading ramp of the plane was down.

"Be all right for us to go on up?" I asked.

"Sure, why not? Your Uncle Ed is expecting us."

I had just put my foot on the first step when I looked up at the plane. I thought I saw a motion at one of the windows.

"Hold it," I whispered to Brains.

I stepped back down, and Brains and I ducked behind the loading ramp.

"What's up, Operative Three?" he asked.

"I think I saw someone watching us from one of those windows. When I looked up, he pulled the window curtain closed."

We waited there, the silence in that cavelike structure seeming to push down on us. Talk about creepy—that place sure was. After a few moments, we raised our heads very slowly until our eye level was just above the top rail of the ramp.

There was a faint light inside the plane. Then we saw one of the window curtains pushed slowly, carefully back, and a man's face appeared in the window.

It wasn't Uncle Ed, either. It was a man wearing a fez. He had the fiercest pair of moustaches I'd ever seen.

"What do we do now? That guy's spying on us. He thinks we're spying on him."

Brains didn't answer, just kept his eyes glued on Mr. Fez.

"Let's get out of here. We'll wait for Uncle Ed outside."

I started to back away. Brains grabbed my arm.

"I think we should investigate further," he said.

Oh, no, I thought to myself. *Not again, Brains.* I didn't know what that man was doing in that plane, and I didn't have any desire to find out. Apparently Brains did.

"Here's what we'll do, Operative Three. We'll sneak underneath the belly of this plane and make our way back to the tail. We can go up that ladder, then creep across the catwalk until we're right over the door of the plane. Then we'll see if we can hear anything."

Creeps!

"But why, Operative X? Maybe that man has a perfect right to be in that plane."

"And maybe he's a Kassabeban spy. Maybe he's in there sabotaging the plane."

Brains was already moving toward the ladder. There was nothing for me to do but follow, unless I wanted to stay there alone. I surely didn't want to do that. I like crowds at a time like this. Even if it's only a crowd of two.

Brains started up the ladder at the tail of the plane, climbing slowly, step by step. I followed. We reached the catwalk and started moving forward on it. It swayed just enough for the butterflies in my stomach to start revving up.

We reached the spot directly over the open door. We listened. At first we didn't hear a thing. Then we heard conversation, very low at first, but getting louder. Whoever was talking was making his way to the front of the plane. In a moment we could hear two voices quite plainly. There were two men. They were directly underneath us, not more than five feet away.

We couldn't make out what they were saying, though. They were talking in a foreign language—Arabic, I guess.

Next thing we knew, one of the men—that man with the fez—came out of the plane. He stood on the platform just outside the door. He turned around to say something else.

I held my breath. If he looked up, he'd surely see us. He looked up.

A burst of angry words came from Mr. Fez. He shook his fist at us. Then he shouted to someone inside the plane.

Brains and I turned around on that catwalk and started for the rear of the plane as fast as we could go. The catwalk really swayed now as we scrambled along it.

We could hear shouting. The two men had left the

plane and were running alongside it toward the rear, trying to head us off.

We slid down the ladder, our feet just scraping the steps. I started running for the exit. I could hear Brains pounding along right behind me. We were outdistancing our pursuers. I was beginning to feel a little easier when, wham! I tripped over a cable. I went into a dive and hit the concrete floor. When I stopped skidding, my head was resting on a pair of feet.

"Oh, oh, Jimmy Carson," I muttered. "This is it. You've had it."

I finally got up enough nerve to look up.

"Investigator Jimmy Carson, I presume?"

I was looking into the grinning face of my Uncle Ed.

14 Of Steaks and Kings

Uncle Ed lifted me to my feet. The lights stopped popping on and off in my head. I looked around me. The first face I saw was that of Mr. Fez. And close up it didn't look any friendlier than it did from a distance.

"You all right, Jimmy? Hurt yourself anywhere?" Uncle Ed asked.

I took a few gingerly pokes at myself, felt my face, and shook my head.

"Now, what's this all about?" Uncle Ed wanted to know.

Before I could answer, Mr. Fez spurted out about ten thousand words, nodding his head angrily at me and at Brains, who was coming back from the other side of the hangar, where he had finally stopped running.

"I see, I see," Uncle Ed said. I guess he had picked up enough Arabic to understand. Anyway, he shot a few of those foreign words back, and the Kassabeban did what they call a salaam. He bowed low, with the palm of his right hand on his forehead. Uncle Ed returned the gesture, and Mr. Fez headed back to the plane as Brains came up.

"Come on, you two. Let's take off for Crestwood."

Uncle Ed didn't say anything until we left the hangar and got into the car. Then he spoke to us sort of chidingly, but not really bawling us out.

"Good thing I got there when I did. You two shouldn't have crossed the hangar without authorization. He could have turned you two over to the security guards, and then I'd have had a real time trying to spring you."

I shot a quick look at Brains. We both felt a little sheepish. Neither of us had a good story to tell Uncle Ed. Sure we were spying, trying to help out, but just what we were spying for—or on—we'd have had trouble trying to explain.

Brains wasn't too bothered. I could tell by the question he put to Uncle Ed.

"Who is that man, the one wearing the fez, Mr. MacDonald?"

"Now, come off it, Sherlock. Why this 'Mr. MacDonald' stuff? I'm just plain Ed or Mac or Captain Mac."

"All right, sir. I'll call you Uncle Ed, too, if it's all right with you."

"It is, Brains." Uncle Ed clapped his hamlike hand on Brains' shoulder. "That man is the Court Treasurer of Kassabeba. His name is Ferez Malab. He came over with me to handle the financial end of picking up the new plane. He's all right—" Uncle Ed paused—"I think."

Uncle Ed changed the subject. "You didn't get a good look at the plane, did you? I'd have taken you through the ship only I don't know just how welcome you'd be right now. We'll look her over later. She's some job."

"It's as big as a regular jet airliner, isn't it?" I asked.

"Yep. Cost plenty, too. Over five million bucks. And what Ras-Bey has had done to her interior—well, you've just got to see it to believe it. He's had New York's top interior decorator handle her inside. The plane's divided up like an apartment. Bedrooms. A dining room. Big picture windows on each side. Finest of silks and brocades for curtains. It's a flying palace."

"Has it got a refrigerator in it?" I heard myself—or my stomach—asking.

Uncle Ed tossed me a quick glance and chuckled. "Yep, a big one, full of roast-beef sandwiches. I read you loud and clear. We'll pull in at the next restaurant we see. You need filling up and I need filling in on what you two have been up to."

Uncle Ed ordered steaks for all of us. When they came, hot, thick, and medium rare, Uncle Ed put a smile on his face as broad as a barn.

"We don't get food like this in Kassabeba. Long time no beef for me. Lamb, that's what we get—lamb every day. If I stay there much longer, instead of speaking I'll be bleating. Now, then, suppose you tell me what's cooking?"

"The Duke and Jujab are in Crestwood," I answered.

Uncle Ed nodded his head. "I thought those two rascals were headed this way. What have they been doing?"

We told him how they had framed Frothingham.

"You boys working on clearing him?" Uncle Ed asked.

"Oh, yes. A most simple matter," Brains answered calmly.

I shot my eyebrows up at this. I felt a little sore.

"You might have told your partner that you found something to help clear Froth," I said, putting as much sarcasm in my voice as I could.

"But, Jimmy," Brains said. "I thought surely you understood that. You cleared him."

I did? That was news to me. Before I could ask how I'd cleared him, Uncle Ed interrupted.

"Why would those two characters want to frame Froth?"

"So the Duke could become Mrs. Willoughby's chauffeur. That way he could keep an eye on Prince Halam and also search the Rolls."

Uncle Ed looked puzzled. "Why search the Rolls?"

"I feel sure that the Golden Vial is secreted some-where in the Rolls. You know, of course, of the signifi-cance in the coronation ceremony of the Golden Vial," Brains said.

"Sure. Sure. But it couldn't be in this country. There couldn't be any coronation without it."

Brains and I told Uncle Ed about how our suspicions had first been aroused when the Duke had swiped the flower vases in the Rolls. We filled him in on the Duke and Jujab's searching the Rolls with a Geiger counter.

"Hey, maybe you two *are* on to something." He stopped to think. "Wait a great big fat minute . . . I just remembered something."

Uncle Ed stopped to down another hunk of steak. Brains and I were leaning forward, our forks sus-pended in midair, halfway between plate and mouth. Uncle Ed chewed.

"What . . . what do you remember?" Brains and I said almost in the same breath.

"About ten days ago," Uncle Ed said, finally swal-lowing, "I was talking about the coronation with a friend of mine in Ras-Bey's court. He said Ras-Bey's jeweler was making a golden vial—and he wondered why. At the time, I figured Ras-Bey was just giving himself another present. But if what you say about the Duke and Jujab is true. . . ."

Brains chewed mechanically. I could tell from the way he stared into space that things were clicking in his head. Then he said "Ha!" so suddenly I jumped.

"Don't you see?" he said. "This is proof that the Golden Vial—the real one—is no longer in Ras-Bey's possession. When he discovered it was gone, he sent the Duke and Jujab to get it back, and to cover himself in the event that they couldn't retrieve it he ordered another one made up."

"Wait a minute, Brains," said Uncle Ed. "How did the original vial get out of Kassabeba? Ras-Bey slapped a tight embargo on the entire country the day after the old Emir's death. Absolutely nothing was permitted to be shipped out."

"How about the Rolls?" Brains asked. "How did *it* get shipped out?"

"Oh, the Rolls. It was sent to England about two weeks before the Emir died. There had been some mechanics out from England working on it. I understand they said the car would have to be returned to the factory. The men found they couldn't fix it there in Kassabeba."

There was a smile of triumph on Brains' face.

"It all adds up. Don't you see? Didn't you imply in your letter to Jimmy that the old Emir died in mysterious circumstances?"

"That's right, Brains. There is one faction in Kassabeba which thinks Ras-Bey had him done in."

"And if the old Emir suspected such a plot, wouldn't he want to do everything he could to insure Prince Halam's ascending the throne?"

"Certainly. The old Emir loved his son."

"Then here is my theory. A request is sent to England to have mechanics come to Kassabeba to fix the Rolls. The old Emir plans to get the Golden Vial out of the country. Why not have it carefully hidden somewhere in the Rolls? Then, later on, he intends telling the Prince where it is hidden." Brains sat back after delivering his lecture.

"But he died before he could get the word to Halam," Uncle Ed said after thinking awhile. "Brains, I buy your theory all the way. That Golden Vial has just got to be in the Rolls."

"But where?" I cut in. "The Duke and Jujab haven't found it. Not yet, as far as we know."

"That's why we've got to kidnap the Rolls," Brains said. "And now we can. Uncle Ed can drive it for us. You see, sir, we want to search the Rolls, too. But we couldn't very well with the Duke and Jujab watching us. We've got to get that Rolls away from them."

"It will be a pleasure," Uncle Ed said. "All through? Let's get out of here."

He paid the check and we were on our way again. We'd been on the road about half an hour when we noticed a car coming up beside us at a terrific clip. It overhauled us and shot by going seventy or eighty. As fast as it was traveling, there was still no mistake about it.

It was the Silver Ghost. Mrs. Willoughby's white and gold Rolls-Royce.

15 The Search

Three hearts shot downward at the same time. Mine, Brains', and Uncle Ed's. We all had the same thought. Why was the Rolls returning from the Strato-Air plant? Why had it been there?

We all felt there could be only one answer. The Duke and Jujab had found the Golden Vial and had taken it to Ferez Malab.

"I just don't get it," Uncle Ed said. "I thought Ferez could be trusted. At least, I *hoped* so."

"What about the other Kassabeban?" Brains asked. "Do you know him as well as you know Ferez? We saw the two of them together in the plane."

"No, I don't know him as well. His name's Raiba something-or-other. I figured Ras-Bey sent him along to spy on Ferez. That's the way Ras-Bey operates. He has spies spying on his spies. For all I know, Ferez may actually be spying on me, Raiba on Ferez, and both of them on the Duke and Jujab."

"We'll have to check over that Rolls first thing in the morning. If we can get it away from the Duke, Froth ought to be able to tell in a minute whether anything's been taken from it." Brains seemed to be pondering his own statement. "I mean, if there's anything torn up in the car—well, Froth knows that Rolls better than I know my bike."

There wasn't anything we could do that night. It was eleven o'clock when we got home. Mom, Dad, and Ann were waiting up to greet Uncle Ed. That didn't mean they let me stay up, too. Dad greeted me with "James, it's long past your bedtime."

That's all he had to say. I went to bed.

Uncle Ed likes to sleep late. I fumed around waiting for him to wake up and have his breakfast. Finally, about ten-thirty, he came downstairs. Mother fussed around him, making him a big breakfast. When he had finished a thick slice of ham, three eggs, six pieces of toast, and about a dozen cups of black coffee, he stretched. At last he paid some attention to me.

"Well, now," he said, "and what have you got lined up this morning?"

"The Rolls. Remember? We've got to start searching it."

"I'm right with you, Jimmy. Call your partner and tell him we'll pick him up in ten minutes."

Brains answered the phone. He must have been sitting right beside it so Mrs. Ray couldn't get to it first. I started to apologize for being so late, but Brains cut me off.

"That's all right, Operative Three. I feel certain that the delay was caused by your Uncle Ed. I await you. I have a plan already formulated for kidnapping the Rolls."

That was good news. I hadn't been able to dream up a thing.

Brains' plan was a dandy, all right. All it did was put me on the spot again. I was to be the decoy. He had taken one of his mother's small rose vases and wrapped it in aluminum foil. If the Duke was hanging around the garage, I was to take this wrapped-up rose vase, display it in front of the Duke, then whisper to my Uncle Ed. Then I was to take off into the woods.

Brains was sure the Duke would follow me. Then Uncle Ed, Froth, and Brains were to take off in the Rolls, Uncle Ed at the wheel.

Now, wasn't that just fine! Some plan. Good old Jimmy Carson, otherwise known as Chief Sitting Duck.

"You can lose him in the woods, Operative Three," Brains whispered to me as we got out at Mrs. Willoughby's. "Then you can join us."

"Where?"

"Why not the rock quarry again? Sure, they know the spot, but they will think it the last place we'd take the car."

So old Sitting Duck started out to do just what
Brains had suggested. When we walked up to the
garage, I pulled the vase from under my jacket and
whispered into Uncle Ed's ear. He nodded his head.
Out of the corner of my eye I could see the Duke. I
could have sworn he had seen the vase. He was looking smack at us. But he turned away, bent down, and
seemed to be inspecting a tire.

By this time Brains and Uncle Ed had already
started for the house to get Froth. There I stood as
though I were waiting for a bus while the Duke walked
casually around the Rolls kicking tires. What could
I do? Now I really did feel as blockheaded as a wooden
decoy.

Finally an idea switched on in my mind. I picked
up a few acorns and started pegging them in the general direction of the weather vane on top of the garage.
No reaction from my friend. I lowered my target sight.
As the Duke bent over to look at a fourth tire, I
whipped an acorn at the middle of his back.

As he jumped around I scrunched down as if gathering more ammunition. I let the fake vase start to
fall out of my jacket, but not quite. With a quick
snatch, I caught the foil-covered object and ran toward
the shubbery leading to the woods.

Like a rabbit, I ran maybe a hundred feet. I halted
and listened. Sure enough, I heard someone come
crashing through the underbrush. At last His Dukeship
had got my message.

I waited just long enough to see him emerge into a small opening. I turned and ran, making plenty of noise so he'd be sure to follow me.

He followed me, all right, and fast. I had to put on all the steam I had to get far enough ahead of him to find a spot to hide. I hid in a tree. I scampered up it just moments before the Duke came crashing through the underbrush.

He stopped right under me. He bent his head this way, then that way, listening. If he'd ever looked up that tree . . . but he didn't, thank goodness. After a few minutes, he headed back for the house. I waited long enough to be sure he couldn't hear me any longer, then cut through the woods toward the rock quarry.

Believe me, I hadn't expected to return to that scene so soon. I still remembered the Duke and Jujab springing at me.

By the time I reached the quarry the search was already under way. Uncle Ed was doing the bossing, Brains the advising, Froth the working.

The Rolls was jacked up in the front, and Froth was taking off the right front wheel.

"Can't tell, Jimmy," Uncle Ed said when he noticed my questioning look. "That vial is small enough to be concealed in a tire. It could be taped to the inside. We can't overlook a thing."

All four tires came off. Inner tubes were taken out. The tire casings were carefully examined.

No vial.

The seats came out. We felt them carefully. There was nothing there. If that vial was hidden in the Rolls, it was one fine job of concealment.

We looked into the engine. We banged pipes. We even probed around the gasoline tank, and the oil intake valve. We looked over every inch of that car.

"Give up, Sherlock?" Uncle Ed asked Brains.

Brains' shoulders sagged. "It's got to be in there," he said stubbornly. "We've got to find it."

"Sure, sure," Uncle Ed said consolingly. "But we haven't been able to find it. Neither the Duke nor Jujab has been able to, either. What's the matter, Froth? See something?"

Froth had been staring at the Rolls' engine for the last couple of minutes like a man in a trance.

"There's something . . . something . . ." he murmured.

He raised his hands in a gesture of complete despair. "Oh, dash it! This entire affair has me so upset I'm in a fog." He closed the "bonnet," as he called it.

"I think we had better return the car. Madame may need it," he sighed.

That's what we did. I was the last one to climb in the Rolls. Just before I did I looked up at the cliff I'd been dangling head down from a couple of days before. I had to suppress a gasp. Poking through the brush was the walrus-moustached face of Ferez Malab. He had been watching our every move.

I waited until we were out of the quarry before telling Brains and Uncle Ed about spotting Ferez.

"Guess he must be spying on me," Uncle Ed said. "Now he must know we're after the Golden Vial, too."

I wondered where Ferez fitted into the picture. Whatever he was up to, I didn't see how it would help us find that vial any sooner, if we were to find it at all. And a kingdom hung on our turning it up soon.

We were a sad group as we drove back to the Willoughby garage. The Duke was there, and the look he gave us was intended to bury us right then and there. We were too disheartened to care.

We climbed into Uncle Ed's rented car. I noticed that I was still holding the foil-covered rose vase. It certainly represented a good plan gone wrong. I chucked it into the backseat. We headed back to town.

"What's the next move, Brains?" Uncle Ed asked.

"We must continue our search. The firm of Benton and Carson refuses to concede defeat."

Fine, I thought to myself. *Just dandy.* But how far can the firm of Benton and Carson go? I was ready to give up, but I knew Brains wasn't. And I knew I'd go right along with him to the bitter end.

That end couldn't be far away, either. The coronation was to take place the next day, Friday.

Uncle Ed let us out at the crime lab. He had some calls to make to Strato-Air Aircraft. He said he'd be available later on in the day if we came up with any new ideas.

Brains jolted me with his next remark.

"Operative Three, do you think you could persuade

our friend Lew Jarman to meet us at the police station within the next hour?"

"I guess so, if he's at the paper. He may be out on a story."

"Go to the *Ledger*. If he's there, telephone me. I will join you at the police station."

"Okay. Fine." I started to walk away. *Hold it,* I said to myself and turned back to Brains.

"What's this all about, Operative X? Why the police station?"

Brains sighed. "While I figure out our next move in locating the Golden Vial, we might as well clear Froth of the hit-and-run charges against him."

16 Froth Is Freed

Luck was with me. Lew Jarman was at his desk in the *Ledger* City Room.

"Be with you in a minute, Jimmy. Soon as I finish knocking out this story."

I sat down at an empty desk next to Lew's. His fingers flew over the typewriter. He was a good typist—fast, too. When he finished the story, he yanked the paper out of his battered typewriter and attacked it with a heavy black pencil. He made some changes, corrected some typographical errors—he called them "typos"—and took the story up to the City Desk.

"That's it for today," he said when he came back. "Deadline for copy closes in five minutes. Unless something big breaks, I'm at your service. What can I do for you?"

"Brains wants to see you. He wants to know if you could come with me and meet him outside the police station."

"Sure I can, Jim. What's up, anyway?"

"We've got enough evidence to clear Frothingham— you know, Mrs. Willoughby's chauffeur."

"Swell, Jimmy. That's fine. Tell me about it."

I stalled. Even though Brains had told me that I was the one who had dug up the evidence to clear Froth, I wasn't too clear on just what it was I had done. I didn't want to admit this to Lew, though. There was no reason for him to know that Brains was keeping me in the dark. I felt a little embarrassed.

"Let's wait until we see Brains," I stalled. "I've got to call him. All right if I use one of these phones?"

"Be my guest, Jimmy."

The police station was just up Main Street one block and round the corner on Liberty Square. Brains said he'd meet us in ten minutes.

"Let me get a 'good-night' from the City Editor and we'll be on our way."

Sounds kind of funny for a person to ask for a goodnight in the middle of the afternoon. But that's how reporters sign off when they quit work.

We got to the police station before Brains did, but not by much. Looking up Franklin Avenue, I could see him, bent over the handlebars of his bicycle like a grasshopper, his knees flashing up and down. There was a package in the basket of his bike.

When he arrived, we held a short conference before going into the police station. We told Lew about the hit-and-run victim's being Jujab.

"You ought to see him. For a man hit by an automobile, he sure is spry. More like an acrobat than somebody who was supposed to be clobbered by an automobile," I said, filling him in about seeing Jujab around Mrs. Willoughby's and at Turner's rock quarry.

"Fine, fine, Jimmy. But what makes you think this other fellow was the driver, the one you call the Duke?"

I looked at Brains. It was time for him to start carrying the ball. He took it beautifully.

"I feel sure I can establish that beyond any reasonable doubt," Brains said.

"Proceed, Brains. I'm lending you all my ears," Lew came back.

"To do so, let's go back to the time immediately after the accident. My partner followed the police car out to the Willoughby estate. He was there half an hour after the accident. On his way to the garage he saw a chauffeur's cap in the driveway. This one." Brains pulled the red-stained chauffeur's cap out of the box he had with him.

"How did it happen to be lying at the side of the driveway? My theory is that the wearer of the cap lost it in his hurry to get away. Perhaps he heard someone coming out of the house and bolted before he could be spotted."

"Sounds reasonable," Lew said.

"Later the impostor, the man posing as Froth, realized how important that cap could be as evidence. He knew that the cap could lead directly to him."

"And how could that happen?"

"In two ways. Observe."

He handed the cap to Lew.

"You will notice that the sweatband has a faint reddish stain? My partner thought at first the stain was blood. I have determined it is a dye."

"I'm following you, Brains," Lew cut in, "but don't give me too many hurdles to jump."

Brains told Lew how I'd been attacked on leaving Mrs. Willoughby's and how my attacker had tried to retrieve the cap.

"And why had the cap become so important to the attacker?" Brains asked.

"I'll bite. Why?" Lew asked.

"For two reasons."

Brains reached in his pocket and pulled out a Kleenex. He unfolded it and displayed two red hairs and two blond ones.

"These hairs were secured for me by my partner at grave personal risk."

"Hey, I got you four red hairs. Only two of those are red," I blurted out.

"Precisely. Through chemical analysis, I examined two of the red hairs. They lost their reddish coloring, proving they had been dyed. Next, I ran a chemical test on a piece of the sweatband. The same dye had stained it. Obviously the wearer of the cap had only recently dyed his hair—a flaming red. Some of the dye faded onto the sweatband."

That crazy-colored hair of the Duke's flashed before my eyes. "Sure," I said. "Sure. The Duke's hair must have come out of a bottle."

Brains frowned at my interruption.

"The Duke, hair recently dyed, was wearing Froth's cap. Therefore, he was the driver of the Rolls at the time of the accident."

Lew thought for a minute. "Good theory, Brains. I'm inclined to go along with you. But I just wonder if your evidence is sufficient to convince the police."

"Ah, but there is more." Brains smiled triumphantly. He had another card up his sleeve.

"Jimmy examined the cap in great haste. The reddish stain was all he saw. It was enough for him to realize he had discovered an important clue. When I examined the cap, I made a further discovery. One that should convince anyone."

Brains took the cap back from Lew. He turned the sweatband back and pulled out a strip of folded paper which had been inserted between the sweatband and the felt of the cap. You know, when a cap or a hat is too big, sometimes people fold up a narrow strip of paper and line the sweatband with it. Makes the hat fit more tightly.

"You know what a large head Froth has. Obviously the person who stole the cap had a head much smaller."

"Sure, Brains, sure. I follow you. But how do you know that it was the Duke whose head was smaller? Could have been anyone."

"Please examine the paper used to line the cap." Brains unfolded it.

Lew and I almost butted heads looking at the paper.

"Looks like an airline schedule to me," I said.

"It is," Lew said.

"Notice the principal language the schedule is written in. Aren't those Arabic characters?"

"By golly, Brains, I believe they are," Lew said.

"Look at the bottom of the page. The name of the airline."

This time I could read the words, printed small and in English.

"Asia Minor–Libyan Airways."

"The airline that serves Kassabeba. It originates in Khartoum and flies a regular schedule to England and America. And who do we know in Crestwood who has recently come from Kassabeba?"

"The Duke and Jujab," I said excitedly.

"Correct. Now, Lew, do you think we have sufficient evidence to clear Frothingham?"

"I'd clear him. I know that. I think maybe the police will go along, too."

"Let's find out." Brains headed into the police station. Lew and I were right behind.

Sergeant Hawkins was the desk duty officer. Officer McKeon was in the squad room. Sergeant Hawkins called him out and Brains went over the story again. Just to show you how thorough my partner is, he had one more clincher to his argument.

"If you have any doubt about my analysis, I have had my findings checked by Professor Abrams. He is head of the chemistry department of Crestwood College. Here is his affidavit saying my procedure was correct and my conclusions are accurate."

That did it. Sergeant Hawkins looked at Brains in awe. Officer McKeon paid Brains an even greater compliment.

"Hope you join the force someday, young fellow."

"Then we have convinced you of Froth's innocence beyond a reasonable doubt?"

"One or two things I want to check out," Officer McKeon said. "I'd like a look at the phony hit-and-run victim. Then a word with the Duke, as you call him, is in order. But for me, you can tell Frothingham I'm sure he'll have his license back soon."

"Thank you very much," Brains said.

I added my thanks and we left.

Outside the police station, Lew stopped us.

"Good work, boys. That's as good a job of sleuthing and wrapping up the loose ends as I've ever seen. But there's more to this than you've told so far. I know Prince Halam is here. I interviewed him yesterday. But what are those other two characters doing here? There's a bigger story in this than Froth's being framed. How about giving out some more?"

Brains shook his head. "We can't just now, Lew. We're right on the verge of breaking the mystery, but there's one small matter we must still clear up."

Small matter? Finding that vase was no small matter and Brains knew it.

17 There's Many a Slip

Saturday was a grim day. Not just because it was cloudy with drizzles every hour on the hour, but because our spirits were just as gray. I was in the crime lab with Brains. We had heard radio reports, brief ones, about the coronation in Kassabeba. It had taken place. Ras-Bey had ascended the throne.

The reports were confusing. It seems there had been some trouble right at the end of the ceremony. No one knew what had happened. Censorship had been clamped on tight soon after the coronation was over. No one was able to tell just what the state of affairs was with the new government. That's what the radio was saying, anyway.

Brains and I saw Uncle Ed right after we heard the reports. There wasn't much he could add.

"I've tried to get through by telephone, but every line into Kassabeba is frozen for official business only."

Prince Halam was with Uncle Ed.

"I talked to our ambassador in London," he said. "But he's as much in the dark as we are. He hasn't been able to get through, either. Something's very wrong when the ambassador can't get through to his own country."

"Perhaps we'll know more about it tomorrow," Brains suggested.

We were all looking forward to Sunday afternoon. A television network had announced a special showing of the coronation over a nationwide hookup for two o'clock Sunday afternoon. They'd had a reporting and camera crew in Kassabeba to record the colorful, historic event. They'd been plugging the special telecast all week.

They had given it a big buildup, all right. The film was going to be edited in flight from Kassabeba to New York. They had plenty of time, because Kassabeban time is ten hours ahead of us. When it's getting to be night there, daylight of the same day is just beginning to start here.

"I'll have to get out of here right after the broadcast," Uncle Ed said. "We're taking off just before midnight for Kassabeba. The crew is all ready. The plane's having its final check-out as soon as I get to Langston. We'll be in Kassabeba late Monday afternoon. Have to make one stop for refueling."

"I wish I were going along," Prince Halam said.

"So do I, Halam. But . . . too dangerous."

"Yes, I know," the Prince said sadly.

Uncle Ed and the Prince headed back for Mrs. Willoughby's. Brains went back to the crime lab. His face was long and I knew how bad he felt. It looked as if this time the firm of Benton and Carson wasn't going to come through. Maybe we'd better cross out "international" on our business cards. I hinted as much, trying to cheer Brains up.

"We can't win 'em all, Operative X," I said. "And this one was tricky, with all this foreign stuff."

"We still aren't defeated," he replied fiercely. "I'll think of something."

He'd have to think mighty fast. Uncle Ed was pulling out. The coronation was over. Halam was still just a Crestwood College boy.

Right now I had to think about my paper route. Not only think about it, but do it.

One cheerful note brightened up my Saturday afternoon. I was coming back from the paper route when I heard a car horn honking behind me. It wasn't the *beep-beep* of the horns in today's cars. It was a Klaxon and made a sound like *Ah—ooo—ga! Ah—ooo—ga*.

I looked over my shoulder. It was the white Rolls. And Froth was at the wheel!

He pulled up for a quick bit of chitchat. The first thing he did was to pull his driver's license from his wallet and display it proudly.

"It was returned to me just after lunch. Officer McKeon brought it back."

"Did he arrest the Duke and Jujab?"

"No, James. They have disappeared. We searched the grounds, and we searched the apartment above the garage. Those two have fled."

"Well, getting them out of the way is one good thing. But if Officer McKeon wants them, he'll catch them. Gee, Froth, I'm sure glad you're in the clear."

"Thanks to the firm of Benton and Carson. I am deeply indebted to you boys. Officer McKeon told me how you had solved the mystery. I'm looking forward to a whopping big bill. Your fee should be a large one for such ripping good work."

He waved his hand and drove off.

Froth's freedom, his friendship, and justice was the only fee we wanted.

Sunday afternoon about one-thirty found quite a gathering in Mrs. Willoughby's music room. My mother was there; Dad was out playing golf. Professor and Mrs. Benton were there, along with Prince Halam, Uncle Ed, Brains, Frothingham, and me.

Mrs. Willoughby was fluttering around, chattering away.

"Oh, I'm so excited! Imagine, we're going to see the coronation. Actually view it on the telly."

The English call TV the telly. Mrs. W. used lots of English expressions.

"Ah, me, Prince Halam, you poor, dear boy. It's so sad. We should be watching you."

The maid, Harriet, brought in tea and something Mrs. W. called scones. They're flat, round cakes. They're not too bad, but I like my mother's cookies better.

At five minutes to two we turned the set on. Everyone leaned forward, waiting. Silence fell over the room. Even Mrs. Willoughby stopped chattering, although she did keep rummaging in that crazy beaded bag for green gumdrops.

Presently the program that had been on faded from view. The TV went blank for a few seconds, and then the screen was filled with horsemen, dashing madly through the picture. The background showed long, low white buildings, with funny-shaped towers—minarets, I think they're called—rising from the corners of these buildings. Then the announcer's voice came in.

"You are about to witness one of the most colorful and exciting ceremonies of the Near East. The setting is the oil-rich country of Kassabeba. We are to see the coronation of a new Emir, Kalib Al Mene Ben Ras-Bey. He is more familiarly known as Ras-Bey.

"Since early morning there has been an endless round of feasting, parading, exhibitions of horsemanship, and other ancient and traditional ceremonies. . . ."

We watched as desert tribesmen, standing in their stirrups, galloped by. Some of them brandished rifles high over their heads. Others carried long, wicked-looking spears with tiny pennants tied to their tips.

The scene changed. Two tanks rumbled by.

"Our armored force," Halam said with a smile.

Then there was an overhead shot. Four small fighter planes came over in tight formation.

In the darkness of the room, lighted only by the TV's picture tube, I glanced at Brains. He wasn't missing a thing. His eyes were glued to that screen.

"And now we come to the highlight of the coronation," the announcer said. "The symbolic ceremony wherein the ascending Emir sips the Pure Water of Life with the lowliest beggar in the kingdom."

The camera came in for a tight close-up of Ras-Bey. In front of him stood a man in tatters. You never saw such a pitiful figure. He was all rags. I knew, though, that he was probably a close friend of Ras-Bey or a relative, and in about three minutes he'd be a beggar no longer but a very rich man.

Once this beggar sipped the Pure Water of Life with Ras-Bey, he would receive enough riches to allow him to live in luxury the rest of his life.

"Now you see Ras-Bey holding high the Golden Vial containing the Pure Water of Life."

We saw it, all right. It looked just like a small rose vase. It was about ten inches long, narrow, with a base the size of half a dollar and the flared top only a little bigger.

The beggar sipped from the Golden Vial. He handed it to Ras-Bey. Ras-Bey sipped.

"Now the crowd is hailing their new Emir," the announcer stated. I'm glad he told me. It sounded more like a bunch of ghosts wailing.

The camera pulled back for a long shot of the crowd. The funny sound had stopped and it didn't look to any of us as if the crowd was hurrahing.

The people were silent. All eyes were still on Ras-Bey and the beggar. Now a chant, low at first, then rising, as if the crowd were angry, began to drown out the announcer's voice. The camera switched back for another tight close-up of Ras-Bey and the beggar.

Both looked confused. Both looked startled and scared.

"What are they saying? What are they shouting?" Uncle Ed asked.

"I can't get it all. There's so much shouting. But they're calling out 'stone' and 'light' and 'wisdom.'" The Prince looked puzzled. He turned toward Brains as if to ask a question.

Brains had leaped out of his seat. His nose was only inches from the TV screen.

"They haven't got it!" Brains shouted. "They haven't got the Golden Vial. Not the real one!"

"Ladies and gentlemen," the announcer cut in. "There seems to be some confusion. We don't know what is going on. The crowd has grown angry. It is closing in. The people are menacing the new Emir. . . . We will get back to you as soon as we find out what has caused the confusion."

The screen went blank momentarily. A man sitting in a studio came on the screen. He had a lot to say about the trouble the camera crew had in getting the film out. Then he ended: "But in any event, you have been a witness to one of the most exciting, most colorful of all ceremonies wherein a new ruler ascends the throne. You have seen Ras-Bey become the new ruler of Kassabeba."

The station did its sign-off and a commercial came on. Brains snapped off the set.

"We have not!" he said. His voice was high with excitement. "We haven't seen a new Emir crowned. Halam, you've still got a chance at the throne."

"Now, what's this all about?" Uncle Ed interrupted.

"Yes, yes," the women said. "What has gone wrong?"

Brains grabbed the Prince by his shoulders.

"Think, Prince Halam! Think! What do the words 'stone' and 'light' and 'wisdom' mean to you?"

I thought my partner had flipped. But then I remembered those were the words the Prince had translated. We all crowded around Brains and the Prince.

The Prince shook his head back and forth, trying to spark his memory. You could see from the expression on his face that he almost had it.

"Wait!" the Prince shouted and tore out of the room.

He was back in a flash, waving a piece of paper over his head. Halam took a deep breath to calm himself down. "I have puzzled over this part of my father's last letter to me many times. Let me read it to you."

In a slow, firm voice, stressing every word, Halam read aloud: " 'If ill should befall our beloved land, remember you are the true son of light and wisdom. Your claim shall be as strong as stone. A trusted one shall help you.' "

We all looked blankly at Halam—all except Brains.

"I know what should have happened," my partner said. "The beggar is supposed to take the Stone of Light and Wisdom from the base of the vial and hand it to Ras-Bey. Sipping the Pure Water of Life isn't enough. The stone is the symbol that the Emir gains his guidance from the people. Until he gets the stone, he cannot rule. The beggar didn't give Ras-Bey the stone! He didn't because he couldn't! He didn't have the original Golden Vial. It must still be in the Rolls!"

"Yeah! Yeah!" I yelped, nodding my head up and down. "Halam's father must have been trying to tell him about the Stone of Light and Wisdom in the letter. But I still don't get it. When Ras-Bey had that phony Golden Vial made, why didn't he have a fake Stone of Wisdom put in it?"

"He didn't know . . . he couldn't have known that any such stone existed," the Prince explained. "You see, before he began his drive to take over Kassabeba, Ras-Bey was only the chieftain of a nomadic tribe roaming the remote countryside. Neither he nor any of the men who helped him fight his way to power had any contact with the civilized life of the court and the great cities. They are all powerful but uneducated men.

When he finally did take over and moved into the palace, he drove out or frightened away everyone connected with my father's reign who could have told him about the Stone of Light and Wisdom."

"Ras-Bey made the mistake many would-be tyrants have made in the past," broke in Professor Benton excitedly. This kind of thing was right up his alley. "He thought that force alone could conquer. He forgot that—"

Then Brains interrupted his own father. That will show you how worked up Brains was.

"There's no time to lose," he said, his voice crackling. "Sir," he added, glancing at his dad. Then he swung around to me.

"Jimmy! Quickly—to the apartment over the garage. Perhaps the Duke and Jujab left in such a hurry they forgot to take that black box with the dial on it. See if it's still there!"

18 Eureka!

We all piled out of the music room like a parade doing double time. Brains was the Pied Piper in the lead. I was right behind him. Then came Uncle Ed and Frothingham. Bringing up the rear were the Prince, Professor Benton, and the ladies.

We sprinted across the driveway as if the garage was on fire.

"Back the Rolls out, Froth!" Brains ordered. "Up those stairs, Jimmy! Find that Geiger counter."

Up the stairs I shot. I glanced quickly around the rooms the Duke had just vacated. He had left them in a hurry. The rooms looked as if a small tornado had hit them. Drawers hung open from the chest; all the furniture looked topsy-turvy. I could hear Brains shouting, "Hurry up, Jimmy! Hurry!"

I finally found the thing—the Geiger counter—stuck under a pile of dirty laundry in the clothes closet in the bedroom. When I got downstairs, it looked like the Rolls was being torn apart.

The hood of the car was open. Froth and Uncle Ed were bent over the engine, one on either side, tapping and thumping away like mad.

Professor Benton, my mother, and Brains' mother had taken out the seat cushions and were beating them with their fists. Mrs. Willoughby stood on the sidelines, frantically waving her feather snake and saying, "Hurry, hurry, hurry along."

The Prince was looking on as if everyone had gone mad.

"Here's your black box," I said.

Brains took it. He started at the back of the Rolls. He moved forward, testing every part of that car inch by inch.

After fifteen frantic minutes, with no results, Professor Benton called a halt.

"Just a moment, Barclay," he said to Brains. "Perhaps if you would enlighten us, we could approach this task more scientifically. We know we're looking for a small, vase-shaped vial. But why the Geiger counter? It is not sensitive to gold."

Brains stopped moving around with the box.

"When I went to Middlebury last week, I found several long, detailed stories in the London *Times* about the coronation of the Prince's father. That coronation took place the last three days of August, forty-eight years ago."

I remembered then. August, the Prince had told us, was the month they called the Season of the Golden Cheese.

"Proceed with your explanation, Barclay."

"The *Times* stories went into the history of the Golden Vial. It seems that about two hundred years ago a small phosphorescent stone was found by a wandering tribesman deep in the Kassabeban mountains. It gave off a brilliant glow in the dark. He took it to the then-reigning Emir. A small cavity was cut into the base of the Golden Vial and the stone placed in it. Presentation of the Stone of Light and Wisdom became a part, the final part, of the ceremony whenever a new Emir was crowned."

"Phosphorescent minerals are quite common, Barclay, but they are not usually radioactive, are they? Why are we using a Geiger counter?" Professor Benton asked.

"When I learned the other day that the Duke and Jujab had been using a Geiger counter in their search of the Rolls, I immediately wondered why. As you yourself pointed out, sir, gold is not radioactive and will not cause a Geiger counter to react. The Stone of Light and Wisdom I knew to be hidden in the true Golden Vial was the only other possible source of radiation. A check of a volume on middle eastern geological formations showed that traces of certain radioactive uranium salts had been found in the mountains of Kassabeba. The probability seemed good that the Stone of Light and Wisdom contained some of those salts."

"Well," said Uncle Ed, "if there's anything radioactive hidden in this Rolls, it must be covered with lead. You're not getting a peep out of that Geiger counter."

Brains was standing in front of the Rolls now. He was staring at the car's radiator. Suddenly his face lit up and flashed like a Roman candle.

"Eureka! Eureka!" Brains shouted and started jumping up and down.

We all crowded around Brains.

"What have you found? Where is it?"

"In the radiator," Brains said. Then he turned to Froth.

"Froth, what year did you say this car was made?"

"The year was 1925—the last year Rolls made the Silver Ghost model."

"Then I'm right," Brains said. "I have found it. I've found where the Golden Vial must be located."

He looked at all of us triumphantly. We all looked at him like dumb bunnies.

"Take a good look at that radiator, Froth. You should have noticed this yourself with your great interest in the Rolls-Royce."

Frothingham peered intently at the radiator. He looked it up and down. He even patted it. He turned to Brains, a questioning expression on his face.

"Froth, you surprise me. When I was at State U.'s library in Middlebury, I also did some research into the history of the Rolls-Royce."

"Yes, Barclay," Professor Benton said impatiently. "Get to the point."

"I discovered that from the inception of the Rolls-Royce, from the first car made to the cars made today, there has been but one small change in the Rolls' radiator."

Brains paused. He liked to build up to what he called "dramatic effect."

"That change was made upon the death of the second partner of the firm. Charles Henry Rolls died flying his own Wright airplane in 1910. Sir Henry Royce died in 1933. Upon his death, the directors of the company, after solemn deliberation, decided to change the two big entwined *R*'s on the radiator from red enamel to mourning black."

Brains looked around as if he expected everyone to applaud. Only Mrs. W. spoke. "Have a gumdrop, dear boy," she said. "Good for brain energy." Brains took one, popped it in his mouth, and went on.

"You will note that the two *R*'s on this Rolls are black. But this car was made in 1925, eight years before the death of Sir Henry. Therefore, the *R*'s on this car should be *red*. The original radiator had been replaced. Why?"

"Why?" I asked.

"So that something could be concealed in the new radiator."

"The Golden Vial!" I whooped.

"You are right. So, I believe if we hold the Geiger counter close to the radiator, we should get a definite reaction."

We did hold the Geiger counter against the radiator. It didn't react.

Oh, there was a faint click—very faint. Then nothing. After a few suspenseful moments, the counter gave out with another feeble click.

Everyone looked at Brains. He was nearing the panic stage.

"It's just got to be there," he shouted frantically.

With that, he unscrewed the radiator cap.

Wow!

That Geiger counter started clacking away like those funny false teeth you wind up that go yakkity-yak.

"I told you! I told you!" Brains was triumphant again.

The Geiger counter continued to clatter way.

"We'll have to take the radiator off," Uncle Ed said. "Get the tools, Froth."

Everyone was beginning to get a little frantic now. Mrs. Willoughby was shooting green gumdrops into her mouth like BB's from an air rifle.

Froth and Uncle Ed went to work on the radiator. They had it off in a small-sized jiffy. They stood it on the ground. Brains took the Geiger counter and held it to the front. No response. He placed it to the rear of the radiator. Again, nothing.

When he placed it directly over the top of the radiator, over the opening the water goes in, that Geiger counter really gave out.

"The Golden Vial must be inside the radiator," Brains said.

"Not necessarily, Brains," Uncle Ed said. "If the vial is enclosed in a lead pipe, then the Geiger counter would react once any opening was made leading to that pipe. It might be inside one of those pipes leading from the radiator to the engine."

Froth had been silent during this discussion. Now he spoke up.

"The other day, when we took the Rolls to the quarry to search it, you, Mr. MacDonald, asked me if I had noticed anything, because I had been staring at the engine for so long. Well, something *didn't* look right, but I couldn't have told you what. 'S'matter of fact, I thought I was beginning to go daft and hadn't seen anything at all. But now something *does* look strange."

"What does?"

"This overflow pipe. Here."

We all crowded around. The overflow pipe, Froth explained, was a lead tube running underneath the outer casing from the top of the radiator and down the side to the ground. If you overfilled the radiator, the water ran out of the pipe instead of spilling all over the gleaming metal on the top of the radiator.

"Jeepers!" I said. I hadn't said anything for a long time, which was unusual. "I've never seen an overflow pipe like that before."

The pipe started out at the radiator cap as a narrow tube about a half inch thick. It stayed that size all the way to where it bent and started down the side of the radiator. Right there, it seemed to become *two* tubes. The original half-inch one kept going right on down the side of the radiator, but behind it was another tube, much larger, that was almost hidden in a hollow in the radiator body. If the radiator had been in its proper position on the front of the Rolls, that hidden pipe would have been almost impossible to see. The tiny part of it that showed must have registered on Froth's eye the day we searched the car at the quarry, but not on his brain. You couldn't blame Froth for that, though. Creeps! I'll bet old Henry Royce himself would have missed it.

The little tube and the big one were both made of lead. Uncle Ed had a pocketknife out in about one second and the double tube off the radiator in two. He slit the soft, dull metal of the big tube down the side and peeled it back with a pair of pliers.

There was the Golden Vial!

A cheer went up. We were all dancing up and down. We'd found the Golden Vial. Prince Halam would get his throne after all. Right at that moment we heard a voice from behind us.

"I'll take the Golden Vial."

We turned to see Ferez Malab approaching us from around the garage. The expression on his face showed he meant business.

19 All Hail!

Uncle Ed went into action. As Ferez Malab reached out to take the Golden Vial from Brains, Uncle Ed chopped down on his outstretched arm and grabbed him.

They wrestled about. Ferez was no match for Uncle Ed, though. Uncle Ed had him on the ground, arms pinned down.

Ferez looked up at Prince Halam and spoke to him in Arabic. The Prince replied.

"Release the man, Mr. MacDonald," the Prince commanded. His tone of voice carried a kingly authority, too.

Surprised, Uncle Ed did as he was told.

Ferez Malab arose, brushed his dusty clothes, and smoothed his dignity back on.

"As Treasurer of the Court of Kassabeba and Keeper of the Golden Vial, I command you to hand it over to me."

Brains looked at Prince Halam. Halam nodded his head curtly, commanding Brains to hand the vial over. Brains did.

Ferez Malab took the vial. He knelt at the feet of Prince Halam and said, first in Arabic, then in English, "Hail to you, Prince Halam. Hail to the true Emir of Kassabeba!"

He arose and presented Halam with the Golden Vial.

The ceremony was brief, but it was touching, too. I felt kind of choked up. When I looked around, I could see my mother wiping her eyes. Tears were rolling down Mrs. Willoughby's cheeks.

Jeepers, we'd had sort of a coronation right here in Crestwood, U.S.A.!

The Prince had been standing very tall and king-like, holding the vase like a scepter. Now he looked into the vial, turned it upside down, and peered at it closely.

Ferez smiled quietly and took the vial from Halam's hand. Ferez touched a small gold leaf at the base of the vial. It slid aside, and out into his hand popped the Stone of Light and Wisdom. Ferez handed it to Halam with tears streaming down his cheeks.

The Prince drew himself up once more, getting more kingly than ever.

"Keep it, O wise and faithful counselor to my father. Keep it safely," the Prince said. "We shall return to Kassabeba and restore rightful rule to the people of my country."

Everybody was really happy now.

At first we had thought Ferez Malab was an unmasked enemy. Now it turned out that he was the "trusted one" mentioned in the letter. That's what he had revealed to Halam in Arabic while my Uncle Ed had him pinned down. He was the one who had known the real Golden Vial was missing. He was the one who knew about the Stone of Light and Wisdom. He'd figured that it must have come out in the white Rolls. That was his real reason for coming to the United States, not just to handle the financial end of the new jet purchase.

Everything seemed clear as Lake Carmine's water. But I just had to know one more thing. So I opened my mouth. "If Ras-Bey didn't know about the stone, how come his buddies Duke and Jujab did? After all, they had the Geiger counter. They must have known."

"Aha," said Ferez. "Jujab is the son of a one-time palace goldsmith. As an apprentice in his father's workshop, he would have known of the stone. He had not been an apprentice long when he was found stealing gold from the palace. The Emir banished him and he went abroad, finally returning after many years, not to the capital city, but to Ras-Bey's band in the mountains. The Duke was with him."

"Aha, aha," chirped Brains, going Ferez one "aha" better. "Of course, then Jujab and the Duke must have tricked Ras-Bey into naming someone they wanted as the beggar who would receive the coronation riches, hoping to find the real Golden Vial later."

"Young man, you have a canny mind. You are right. The beggar's gift is veritably a fortune," Ferez said.

Uncle Ed suddenly whacked his hands together to get attention. "We have a show—and what a show— to get on the road.

"Prince Halam," Uncle Ed said, "I can land you in Kassabeba by midafternoon tomorrow. Can you get ready to leave at once?"

The Prince, all smiles now, just grinned. "As you say in America, 'You betcha my boots!'"

"I'll help you get ready. Must pack . . . must pack! Right away!" Mrs. Willoughby said excitedly.

"That won't take long, Madame Willoughby. I really didn't unpack, since I knew I'd be moving over to the college next week."

"Oh, college, college. Now you can't go. Or can you? Can you come back and enter Crestwood College?" Mrs. W. asked.

"That, Madame, will depend entirely on my duties and responsibilities as the Emir of my people. I would dearly love to, however. I feel you are all my friends. Especially you two."

The Prince came over to where Brains and I were standing and put his arms around our shoulders.

I felt as if I was being made a knight.

"Well, let's get moving," Uncle Ed said. "We have a long drive ahead of us."

"I wonder, Mr. MacDonald," Froth asked, "if we could restore this radiator to its proper position. I should deem it a great honor if I could drive the Prince to Langston and help escort him aboard the plane."

"Sure thing, Froth. We can do that while the Prince is getting ready. Hey, let's make it a party. Why don't we all go? We can split up. Some in the Rolls, some in my rented job."

Boy, that sounded good to me.

It sounded good to everybody.

"I'll have to stop at your house, Clara," Uncle Ed said to Mom. "Got to pick up my bag. And I want to call Strato-Air and have them run the preflight check-out without me."

Froth and Uncle Ed replaced the radiator. They couldn't put the overflow pipe back on. A new one was needed. But the pipe wasn't essential to the car's operation anyway.

An hour later our princely cavalcade pulled away from the Carson homestead on Maple Street. I was riding with Uncle Ed, Brains, and Professor Benton. Mrs. Benton, my mother, the Prince, Mrs. Willoughby, and Ferez Malab rode in the Rolls with Frothingham.

As I had flopped in the backseat, my right hand flipped and hit something hard. It was the old vase I'd tossed in Uncle Ed's rented car the day before. I didn't know it then, but it was going to come in very, very handy.

We were on the last happy leg of our adventure. Everybody thought we were home free now.

We weren't though. We were heading for trouble. Serious trouble.

20 Touchdown

It was dark by the time we had been on the road for a couple of hours. We could tell we were nearing Langston and the Strato-Air Complex. Searchlights on the airstrips probed and swept the sky. Now and then a light beam would pick out a silvery jet making a night test flight and hold it in its sweeping beam.

Brains and I were sitting in the backseat.

"I wonder what ever happened to the Duke and Jujab," Brains wondered out loud.

"Maybe Officer McKeon picked them up," I said.

"I doubt that. He'd have gotten in touch with us or with Frothingham, if he had."

Uncle Ed twisted his head and spoke out of the side of his mouth.

"What's that about the Duke and Jujab?"

"Just wondering what happened to them," Brains replied.

With that, Uncle Ed braked the car and pulled over to the side of the road.

"I'm glad you mentioned those two," Uncle Ed said. "I'd forgotten all about them, too."

"Why are we stopping, Ed?" Professor Benton asked.

"I think I'd better have a conference with the Prince and Ferez. Right now, too. There's no telling what those two jokers—the Duke and Jujab—might be plotting."

We waited a few minutes and saw the Rolls coming around a curve. Uncle Ed stepped out of the car and waved a flashlight up and down. Froth pulled the Rolls over right behind our car.

Ferez, the Prince, Uncle Ed, Professor Benton, Brains, and I held a conference. Froth stayed behind the wheel of the Rolls.

"Brains here just mentioned the Duke and Jujab," Uncle Ed said, speaking to Ferez. "It suddenly struck me that they might still be plotting some way of trying to get hold of the Golden Vial. Raiba has a pass to the hangar, you know."

"You are quite right, Mr. MacDonald," Ferez said. "They will be desperate now. A rich kingdom is going to be lost to Ras-Bey. And Ras-Bey is a vicious man. When he learns that they have failed to recover the true Golden Vial, he will seek his revenge."

"You think they might try something at the airstrip?"

"Yes," answered Ferez. "When they see Prince Halam boarding the plane, they will know the vial has been found. They will try to get it then."

"But, Mr. MacDonald," Professor Benton cut in. "There are six of us, including Frothingham and the two boys. Surely they wouldn't be able to overpower us."

"They have another ally," Ferez said. "Raiba. He was sent to watch my actions and also to spur the Duke and Jujab in their hunt for the vial. There will be three of them against us. All three are strong and tricky."

A plan was forming in my head. I wasn't ready to spring it yet. I wanted to outline it to Brains first. I touched his arm and pulled him aside.

"Listen, Operative X," I whispered. "What do you think of this plan if we bump into the Duke, Jujab, and their pal?"

I whispered fast for a few minutes. Brains kept nodding his head, agreeing with me.

"Come on, boys," Uncle Ed called. "Let's get moving again."

Back in the car, Uncle Ed just said, "We hope there won't be any trouble, but we've got to be alert for it. Everyone keep his eyes sharply peeled. If there's any sign of those three characters, holler out."

We pulled up at the gate of the Strato-Air Complex. After a few minutes Uncle Ed got us all passed through and we headed for Hangar Ten.

The plane was all fueled and ready to take off.

Uncle Ed spoke to the copilot.

"Roll her out on the strip and warm her up. We want to get out of here fast."

A tractor hooked on to the nose of the jet and towed her out of the hangar. She looked funny, like a big whale being towed by a small crab.

We could hear the whine of the jet's four engines as she warmed up. The whine turned into an earsplitting shriek. Then the motors were cut back to a lower, whistling noise.

"Well, guess this is it," Uncle Ed said. "We're ready."

The Prince shook hands with everyone. Mrs. Willoughby took him in her arms and planted a big smacking kiss on his cheek. He came over to us, once he had freed himself from Mrs. W.'s bearlike hug, and gave us a playful punch in the ribs.

"Next time your Uncle Ed comes over here, I'm going to order him to bring you two back for a visit."

Gosh, wouldn't that be swell!

Just then I spotted a stealthy movement in the darkness just behind us. Brains saw it at the same time. We were all standing at a small gate leading out to the airstrip.

"Uncle Ed," I said in a low voice, "look behind us. I think we're in for it."

Uncle Ed turned quickly. The Duke, Jujab, and Raiba came at us on the run.

"Prince," I said in a hurry. "Take this. They'll think it's the Golden Vial. Just before they close in on us, toss it to me. They'll think I've got it, and you can rush out to the plane.''

Uncle Ed heard me. "Hey, swell idea!"

When the Duke was about ten feet away I let out a holler.

"Hey, Prince. Toss it to me!"

The phony rose vase, wrapped in aluminum foil, came arching through the air. It did look almost exactly like the Golden Vial, if the vial had been wrapped up in aluminum foil, too.

The Prince made a perfect pass. I snatched the vase out of the air.

"I got it! I got it!" I yelled, holding the vase up.

The Duke spotted me and the vase. He swerved toward me without slackening speed.

Just as he was about to grab me, I tossed the vase to Brains. If I do say so myself, it was a neat lateral pass. The Duke lunged toward Brains. Brains passed to me. We kept it up. Brains was a good passer for a sideline strategist. There were no fumbles and no interceptions. The Duke wasn't a very good defensive player. He kept charging back and forth between Brains and me.

As we passed the vase back and forth, we kept moving away from the gate leading to the plane.

The Duke changed his strategy. He shouted orders to Jujab to cover me. He shrieked at Raiba to cover Brains. He got in the middle to intercept.

I took a moment to glance toward the gate. Only the women, Froth, and Professor Benton stood there now.

Then we heard the whine of those four jet engines increase in intensity. The Prince, Ferez, and Uncle Ed had made it. The jet was rolling out on the strip ready for takeoff.

About that time, the Duke must have heard the plane, too. He stopped trying to intercept our rose vase. He knew he had been tricked. He knew they would never take off without the Golden Vial.

Now he started running to the gate. Jujab and Raiba were right behind him.

The three ladies, Froth, and Professor Benton separated on each side of the gate making a path for the three thieves to run through.

The Duke reached the gate in full flight. Just as he was about to pass through it, Mrs. W. unwrapped her feather boa from her neck and threw it in the Duke's face. At almost the same time, Professor Benton stuck out his leg. Fighting feathers, the Duke went sprawling. Jujab landed on top of him. Raiba added to the pileup.

Whistles started blowing. Security guards came running up to the gate. They took over. The Duke, Jujab, and Raiba were led away.

The rest of us stood at the gate. We could see the jet making its takeoff run. Then it was airborne, heading west. When it gained altitude, it circled, came in fast and low over our heads. As the giant plane blasted past us, Uncle Ed dipped its wings in a farewell salute.

When we had all piled into the Rolls a while later,

Mrs. Willoughby insisted that we all come up to the estate for supper to celebrate the return of the Kassabeban throne to its rightful owner. Everybody thought that was a great idea. On our way through Crestwood, we stopped off at 43 Maple Street. I ran in and told my dad to bring our car and get up to Mrs. Willoughby's right away. I didn't try to tell him everything that had happened. We would fill him in later, over supper.

Supper! Creeps! I had forgotten all about that wild Kassabeban in the Willoughby kitchen. Then I relaxed. If he had been helping the Duke and Jujab all along, he must have skipped out when they did. I wouldn't have to face him again.

I asked Mrs. Willoughby about him. She said poor dear Khouri had been forced to help the Duke and Jujab. They had threatened to do something to his relatives back in Kassabeba if he didn't. So he was probably back at his old stand right now, making meatballs wrapped in grape leaves to feed us. I was right. When Harriet, the maid, brought in the huge, steaming platter it was heaped with them. And right behind her, in the kitchen doorway, was Khouri!

I ducked. Then he smiled . . . right at me. I decided then and there I was going to like that supper, grape leaves and all.

Maybe it was because we had solved another tough case and now that it was all over, Brains and I were getting our share of praise, but something made those little lumps of lamb taste pretty good. As Brains said later, "A pat on the back makes anything easier to swallow."

He'd go far someday, that Brains.

Well, I guess that about wraps up the case of the roving Rolls, though there were one or two matters still to be cleared up.

Brains' father learned the next day that the Duke, Jujab, and Raiba had been turned over to authorities of our State Department. They were going to deport them to Kassabeba. There wasn't really any charge they could be held on in this country. I imagine in the end they would have preferred being kept here rather than go back and face the wrath of Ras-Bey.

One afternoon, a couple of days later, I was home. It was right after school. I wanted to get part of my homework done before I went out on my paper route.

Mom came in with a big smile on her face.

"It's a cablegram from Uncle Ed—for you."

A *cablegram! Really big international stuff*, I thought. I ripped the envelope open and began to read.

ALL'S WELL STOP RAS-BEY HAS FLED TO MOUN-
TAIN HIDEOUT STOP PRINCE HALAM TO BE CROWNED
IN TWO DAYS STOP PEOPLE LOVE HIM STOP HE SENDS
THANKS AND BEST WISHES STOP SAME GOES FROM
YOUR UNCLE ED.

That was the end of the cable. I stuffed it in my pocket to show Brains. It would make a nice addition to our files on "the Roving Rolls." We could really stamp the folder "case complete" now.

I sat back, feeling good all over.

The phone rang. Mom answered.

She came upstairs again to my room.

"Better get some more soap, Jimmy. Seems there are some more alligators that need washing."

The emergency message from Brains! What was up now?

Well, I sighed to myself, *here we go again*.

Whitman CLASSICS

Here are some of the best-loved stories of all tim
Delightful ... intriguing ... never-to-be-forgotte
tales that you will read again and again. Sta
your own home library of WHITMAN CLASSIC
so that you'll always have exciting books at you
fingertips.

REG. U.S. PAT. OFF.

Whitman ADVENTURE and MYSTERY Books